I0620605

THE

HARD

SERIES

E/K

. . .

2nd Edition, June 2015
Written by William S. Mitcham
Edited by Sidonie Lailler

Copyright © 2015 William S. Mitcham/Copyright © 2015 Ellis Kross
All rights reserved.
ISBN: 978-0-9905356-9-0

Cover by William S. Mitcham
Book Design by William S. Mitcham
Artwork by William S. Mitcham

This is a work of *fiction*.
Names, characters, places, and incidents
are the products of the author's imagination.
Any resemblance to actual persons, living
or dead, is entirely coincidental.

Printed in the United States of America

Without limiting the rights under copyright reserved above, no part of this publication may
be reproduced, stored in or introduced into a retrieval system, or transmitted, in any form, or by
any means (electronic, mechanical, photocopying, recording, or otherwise), without the prior
written permission of both the copyright owner and the above publisher of this book.

PUBLISHER'S NOTE
This is a work of fiction. Names, characters, places, and incidents either are the product of
the author's imagination or are used fictitiously. Any resemblance to actual persons, living or
dead, business establishments, events, or locales is entirely coincidental.

The scanning, uploading, and distribution of this book via the Internet or via
any other means without the permission of the publisher is illegal and punishable
by law. Your support and respect of the author's rights is appreciated.

. . .

FOREWORD

BEFORE I begin, I would like to make note that the following section contains minor *spoilers*—and if you find them as irritating as I do, you can save yourself the aggravation and turn the page.

Now that I've cleared the air, the first—and perhaps—the most crucial revision to Freeze's story is the title: *Hard Copy*, the first volume of THE HARD series. The screenplay takes place well before the timeline of the novel, *Freeze: A Week With Mr. Hopkins*; in fact, most of the screenplay was snippets of dialogue taken from journalist Renny Jacobson's interview with the reclusive optimist who goes by the name Mr. Hopkins, and then constructed in a more linear fashion of storytelling. The second volume, which I believe bares a more fitting title, *Hard Pressed*, follows a nearly identical structure as the first novel. The second volume is centered around Freeze's biological daughter, Chloe, who—after being viciously attacked late one night in her home—discovers a USB flash drive in her assailant's pocket; and then, from there, the story is told through her point of view, as well as her father's, each story running parallel to one another: Chloe (PRESENT DAY) on the run by a ruthless death squad and Freeze

(FLASHBACKS) on the run from The Company, or better known as JeneCorp. The third and final volume, *Hard Justice*, is mainly based on the second novel, *Freeze: Final Days*. And even though these titles adequately succeed for the novels, I figured—since THE HARD series is considered a collection of screenplays—it was only appropriate to give them "movie" titles. After all, novels will remain in the novel realm. And movies will remain in the movie realm. Think of it like this: one is like oil; and the other is like water. They will not properly mix. And usually, one will always be heavier than the other.

If you have read the novels, then you will notice several changes that have been made throughout the screenplay. Most of them could be easily missed; however, the alteration made to Freeze's daughter, Chloe, is quite significant. Originally, she goes by Anne Roth, a family name handed down to her by her foster parents. In the novel, she is conceived by Leon (Freeze) and Isabel. In the screenplay, she is conceived by a surrogate mother who works for Aerodyne. I decided to change this part of the story because I wanted to create more deception, as well as complexity to Doctor Monaghan, a sleeper character who plays a key role in Leon's development. After Doctor Monaghan tricks Leon into sleeping with her, not only are her true colors revealed, but also Aerodyne's. You're itching to find out why this secretive organization wants Leon's power so badly and when—or if—they harness his power, what will they do with it? Will they use it to solely benefit mankind or will they use it to destroy mankind?

Several other changes were made throughout the story; however, if you haven't read the novel and managed to plow through the spoilers, I strictly recommend—despite the slight variations—reading this screenplay first. I actually encourage you to start here, from where it all began. And if you've already read the book, this is what has become popularized as a prequel. A great deal of interesting ideas are peppered throughout THE HARD series—in a way, a forewarning (even though they're fictitious stories based on the classical myth that we have grown to love). And if you're unaware of the myth, then this is sort of a quick insight into the legendary character, although with several modifications. Nonetheless, they should spark the questions: If you knew the fate of our future—for instance, the typical Doomsday scenarios that we constantly watch in our movies—would you do anything in your power to stop them? Or, would you sit back and let society fall like grains of sand into an hourglass? THE HARD series is a collection of stories that will make you wonder if a bleak future awaits us, especially since we have the accessibility of technology within our fingertips. But there has to be at least a shred of hope. Right? And that's what these stories will give you, just a shred; however, it's up to you, Reader, to take that shred of hope and turn it into an idea that can reshape the course of humanity.

After all, knowing what we know about technology and how one day it could very well control our entire lives—if it hasn't started to already—I believe the questions we not could but *should* be asking ourselves: Are we rewiring ourselves for the future or are we rewiring ourselves to fit whatever is currently acceptable?

— E.K., May 25, 2015

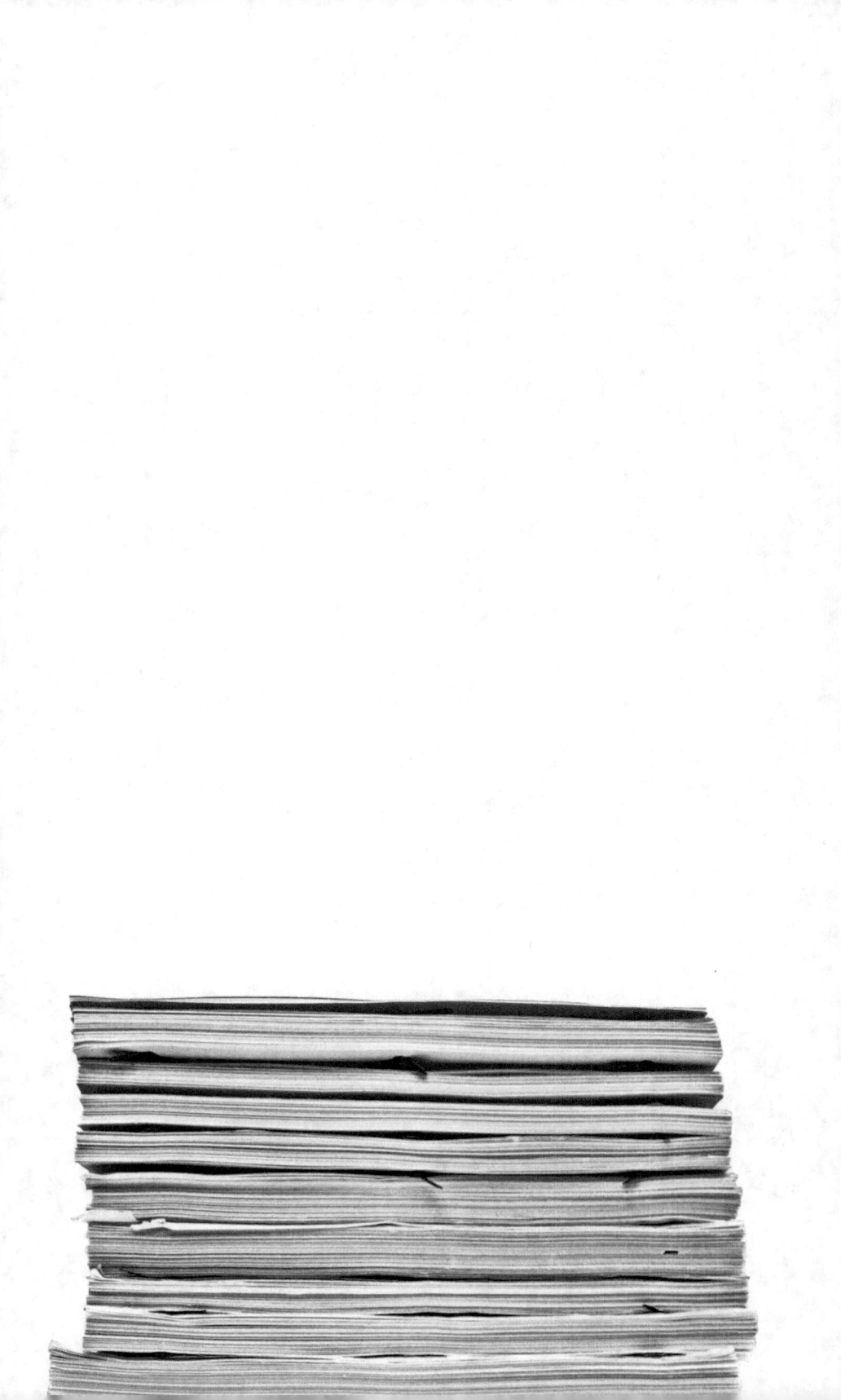

W I L L I A M   S .   M I T C H A M

HARD COPY

HARD COPY

HARD COPY

BLACK SCEEEN

We hear the voice of a young boy over the feeble whistling of wind.

                        BOY'S VOICE (V.O.)
                My father once told me, 'Monsters don't exist.
                The only monsters,' he said, 'are the ones that live
                inside a child's imagination.'

BLACKNESS fades, and so too does the sound of the wind. As the final
whispers of the wind fall into a globe of stark silence, we see a pair of youthful
blue eyes.

INT. GALLERY, LEATHERBY MANOR - DAY

In front of a glass case mounted on top of a wooden perch stands another boy,
MICHAEL, eleven years old.

                        MICHAEL
                My father says they do exist. He talks about them
                while drinking his coffee and watching Morning
                News.

Next to Michael stands the boy behind the voice, young LEON, twelve years old.

In his hand, Leon rubs a glossy black JET stone, as small as a coin, between his
fingertips.

                        LEON
                People do bad things, Michael. Doesn't make
                them monsters.

Michael hangs his head while Leon directs his attention toward the case.

                        LEON (CONT'D)
                My father used to tell me stories about her.
                That's all they were to me. Just stories.

EXT. ALLEYWAY, CRETE, GREECE - DAY - FLASHBACK SEQUENCE

We see a hooded priestess, MEDUSA, 24 years old, moving in SLOW
MOTION through a crowd of pedestrians -- mostly sailors. Her head is lowered,
her gray face disguised underneath the beige cloak. She prowls, almost masterly,
rubbing shoulders with each pedestrian. Unscathed.

> LEON (V.O.)
> Once upon a time, there was a young priestess
> named Medusa.

INT. ATHENA'S TEMPLE - NIGHT - FLASHBACK SEQUENCE

Medusa, a few years younger, attractive, climbs the steep stairs of a temple.
Carefully looks behind her before entering. Then grabs a torch from a holder.
Holds it close.

> LEON (V.O.)
> She was said to be, 'one of the most beautiful
> women in Athens.'

Medusa walks through the open temple. Behind her, a pair of hungry eyes light
up in the darkness. A gargantuan man, POSEIDON, long and wavy hair, chiseled
body, creeps from the shadows.

A frightened Medusa rotates around, face gaping, stumbles. The torch crashes to
the ground, as she scurries away on her hands and knees.

From behind Poseidon, we see the god disrobe.

> LEON (V.O.) (CONT'D)
> One night, Medusa was ravished by the god,
> Poseidon, inside Athena's sacred temple.

EXT. CAVE - NIGHT - FLASHBACK SEQUENCE

Surrounded by a pit of venomous snakes, Medusa -- shivering and crying -- curls
herself into a ball.

> LEON (V.O.)
> Out of pure rage, Athena punished Medusa for
> desecrating her temple by cursing Medusa into a
> creature so hideous that no man would ever look
> upon her ever again...

The goddess, ATHENA, surfaces from a swell of darkness, the snakes slowly parting as she steps forward. Kneels down. Grabs both sides of Medusa's head.

Terrified, Medusa suddenly turns hideous, skin aging like an old woman, snakes sprouting from her scalp.

INT. GALLERY, LEATHERBY MANOR - DAY - PRESENT DAY

Leon focuses on the case; eyes never leaving the artifact inside.

> LEON
> ...And if anyone looked at Medusa, they would be
> turned into stone by her gaze.

EXT. CAVE - NIGHT - FLASHBACK SEQUENCE

A SAILOR treks through a narrow passage near the shore, shining the torch behind a rock face, revealing Medusa's hideous face, her eyes wide and filled with white. Gaping. The sailor turns to stone.

EXT. ALLEYWAY, CRETE, GREECE - DAY - FLASHBACK SEQUENCE

In SLOW MOTION, the mysterious Medusa nudges her head upward, revealing her piercing white eyes underneath the shadows of the hood.

EXT. CAVE - NIGHT - FLASHBACK SEQUENCE

In a pit of darkness, the warrior, PERSEUS, using a rare reflective shield for protection, blindly swings his sword across the neck of Medusa, severing her head....

> LEON (V.O.)
> After spending years in solitude, Medusa finally
> met her match: a great warrior named Perseus...

Medusa's head spins in the air, in SLOW MOTION.

>   LEON (V.O.) (CONT'D)
> ...They said any man who obtained Medusa's
> head could defeat entire armies, even cripple
> worlds.

The head finally hits the ground.

>   LEON (V.O.) (CONT'D)
> Ashamed for the very thing she created, Athena
> hid the head where no man could reach it or so
> she thought...

EXT. DEAD SEA - DAY - FLASHBACK SEQUENCE

A DARK FIGURE stands tall in a desert landscape basking in the redness cast from the Great Sun on the brink of being shrouded by a blanket of ominous clouds.

We get a CLOSER look at the figure: Leon's father, archaeologist, PETER DORSEY, 40's, patchy beard, handsome.

>   MALE VOICE (O.S.)
> There's a storm coming, sir.

Peter looks down at the jet in his palm, pockets it, then turns toward an ARAB approaching from behind -- AK-47 draped over shoulder, body dressed for the desert: loose and yet thin layers that wave in the wind like lush manes.

>   PETER
> This may be the last sunset we'll ever see, Ishmael.

Peter slaps the Arab, ISHMAEL, on the shoulder. Walks away as the wind picks up speed.

>   PETER (CONT'D)
> Take it in.

Ishmael laughs.

ISHMAEL
(in Arabic)
You're just as crazy as they say you are.

PETER
Only worse, brother!

Peter makes his rounds around his TEAM OF WORKERS -- all Arabs -- chiseling away at rocks and boulders among the ruins of a BURIAL SITE.

Gusts of wind cause other WORKERS to flee from the site; however, Peter and his workers tirelessly work despite the looming storm.

INT. GALLERY, LEATHERBY MANOR - DAY - PRESENT DAY

Curious, Michael turns to Leon, whose face is partially revealed behind the case before him.

MICHAEL (O.S.)
What happened to him? Your father?

EXT. DEAD SEA - DAY - FLASHBACK SEQUENCE

The last ray of sunlight pierces through the gray sky and shines upon the edge of a metallic object protruding from the earth.

Peter's partner, a Jewish man, JOSEPH ZAPPIN, around same age as Peter, lanky, narrow face, wide shoulders, frantically clears away the dirt with his hands.

JOSEPH
Peter! Get over here! Fast! I found something!

Brutal winds violently cut across the desert land, nearly destroying the site.

Joseph grabs a BRUSH from his toolset. Brushes the dirt.

PETER
What did you find, Joseph?

The hardened sand clears from the object, exposing the edge of a round object with an engraving of a coiled snake.

                            JOSEPH
                    I don't know...

A gust of wind FLINGS the barricades from the site; a piece of debris comes inches away from striking Peter.

                            ISHMAEL (O.S.)
                    Get out of there!

Ishmael waves down Peter and Joseph.

                            ISHMAEL (CONT'D)
                    We must leave! Now, Peter!

As Peter GRABS Joseph, the earth caves in...

The earth SWALLOWS the bottom half of Peter's body, Peter losing his grip from Joseph. Joseph leaps toward Peter and grabs him by the arm.

                            JOSEPH
                    Peter! I got you!

Joseph pulls on Peter's arm, but Peter resists.

                            PETER
                        (nonchalantly)
                    Joseph, it's all right. Let me go, brother...

INT. GALLERY, LEATHERBY MANOR - DAY - PRESENT DAY

Leon stares at the glass case, a tiny spotlight casting a light on a strange, shriveled head displayed inside; however, we only see half of the face.

EXT. SINKHOLE, DEAD SEA - DAY - FLASHBACK SEQUENCE

Floundering in a puddle of mud, Peter's eyes bolt open. Looks up, only to see a gaping hole at least fifty feet above him. Touches the gash on the side of his forehead. Hisses.

                            JOSEPH (O.S.)
                    Peter! Can you hear me?

Peter attempts to stand but slips in the mud. His injuries: only a few cuts and bruises, as well as a twisted ankle.

> PETER
> Yeah! I'm alive!
> (chortling)
> I can't believe it...

Peter's hand crosses Joseph's chisel protruding from the mud; rips off a piece of his scarf around his neck; wraps it around the edge of the chisel.

Then, he pulls out a lighter from his pocket and lights the scarf on fire.

Curiously, Peter smells the black mud. Recoils from the potent stench. Moves the torch around the massive fissure, which runs like a tight hallway inside the earth.

Then, he moves the torch to the ground where he finds the same object from before. Shines the light on a reflective shield outlined with brass.

Peter wipes away the mud, the snake pattern brought forth in its entirety: the head of the legendary MEDUSA.

The orange light from the torch slowly turns to a soft blue light, which grows around a bend in the wall.

Peter removes the torch from his face; his eyes readjust. Walks toward the pale light, which opens up to a small cave.

EXT. CAVE - DAY - FLASHBACK SEQUENCE

Peter stops at the edge of the cave. Eyes light up with fascination. Mouth gaping. On a rocky mount rests the same strange head...

> PETER
> (in awe)
> Dear God...

> MICHAEL (V.O.)
> You said it was only a story.

INT. GALLERY, LEATHERBY MANOR - DAY - PRESENT DAY

Michael takes a look at the head from a different angle.

> MICHAEL
> I've heard that one drop of her blood can spawn
> the deadliest creatures in the world! I've heard if
> you ingest one of her scales, then you possess --

> LEON (O.S.)
> (vacantly)
> -- Just stories, Michael. Remember.

A strange twinkle in Michael's eye, a grin creeps onto his face. He turns toward the corpse's head preserved inside the special casing. Now, we see the head in its entirety, MEDUSA'S HEAD!

> MICHAEL
> I dare you to eat one.

Leon displays a grin as well.

> LEON
> You're on.

Hesitantly, Leon opens the case, then plucks off one of the rotten scales from Medusa's cheek. Holds it close. The scale looks like an old lady's fingernail.

> LEON (CONT'D)
> Here goes nothing...

Leon sticks the scale on the back of his tongue, then swallows.

> MICHAEL
> So? Do you feel different?

Leon shrugs, then...

He grabs his throat, acts as if he's choking. Falls to floor. Michael, panicky, tends to Young Leon.

> MICHAEL (CONT'D)
> Somebody help!

INT. KITCHEN, LEATHERBY MANOR - CONTINUOUS

Leon's butler, DIEGO, short, slicked back hair, stern in demeanor, turns his head to the sounds of screaming.

> MICHAEL (O.S.)
> Help!

INT. GALLERY, LEATHERBY MANOR - CONTINUOUS

Leon points at his friend, laughs.

> LEON
> You should've seen the look on your face!

Michael kicks Leon in the side. Gives him a Charley Horse.

> MICHAEL
> Not funny.

The door swings open; Diego rushes into the gallery.

> DIEGO
> What did I tell you boys? This room is off limits!

> MICHAEL
> (pointing at Young Leon)
> It was Leon! He dared me!

> DIEGO
> You're in big trouble, Master Dorsey! Big trouble!

Diego picks up Leon by the arm. He notices the door to the glass case is cracked open. He closes it, then guides both Leon and Michael from the gallery.

INT. LEON'S BEDROOM, LEATHERBY MANOR - DAY

Leon watches Michael leave with both of his worried parents.

Michael looks up at the window, sees Leon standing behind it. Leon waves at his friend, but only receives a glare from Michael. Leon then plumps himself on the edge of his bed. Examines the jet in his hand.

EXT. COURTYARD, HIGH SCHOOL - DAY

As Leon, now 17 years old, passes a group of students, his eyes cross a pretty brunette, TAMMY CHESSMAN, carrying a stack of books between her arms.

Both Leon and Tammy share a gaze. Tammy turns away. Smiles. Leon smiles back.

INT. LEON'S BEDROOM, LEATHERBY MANOR - NIGHT

A shirtless Leon brushes his wavy dirty blonde hair in the mirror. Places the comb aside. Checks out his pecks, then his back. He focuses his attention on a piece of loose skin dangling from his shoulder blade. Peels it off. Looks at it closely. The skin is hard and coarse.

INT. KITCHEN, LEATHERBY MANOR - NIGHT

Diego stands in front of Leon, picks a piece of flint from his jacket, then adjusts each sleeve. Straightens the collar on Leon's shirt. Diego comes across a bulge in his breast pocket. Reaches inside. Pulls out the jet.

> DIEGO
> I thought you outgrew superstitions, Master
> Dorsey.

Leon grabs the jet from Diego's hand. Pockets it.

> LEON
> I can use all the luck I can get.

> DIEGO
> I remember my first date, sir. Her name was
> Veronica. She was drop dead gorgeous.

> LEON
> Were you nervous?

> DIEGO
> Petrified.

LEON
(sarcastically)
That makes me feel a lot better.

Diego places his white-gloved hands on the sides of Leon's arms. Squares both shoulders.

DIEGO
Just have fun, Master Dorsey.

EXT. MOVIE THEATRE - NIGHT

In the middle of the audience sit Leon and Tammy. The glow from Quentin Tarantino's "PULP FICTION" reflects off their tranquil faces.

VINCENT (O.S.)
They call it a Royale with cheese.

JULES (O.S.)
Royale with cheese!

Both Leon and Tammy laugh, turn to one another, both smile. Then, they lock hands.

EXT. DRIVE-IN - NIGHT

On the patio sit Leon and Tammy. Leon sips on a milkshake while Tammy nibbles from a french fry; however, they hardly touch their cheeseburgers.

LEON
You know what they call a Quarter Pounder with cheese in Paris?

Tammy laughs, slaps Leon on the shoulder while chewing on the french fry.

LEON AND TAMMY
(at the same time)
A Royale with cheese!

Leon laughs as well.

EXT. PIER - NIGHT

The pale moonlight glistens off the softly beating ripples of the BAY surrounding the outskirts of the coastal city.

Leon caresses the jet between his fingertips. A pale light faintly glistens <u>inside</u> the blackness of the jet.

> TAMMY
> (looking at the jet)
> What is it?

> LEON
> It's a jet.

Leon removes his eyes from the jet for a moment, looks into Tammy's moonlit eyes.

> LEON (CONT'D)
> It belonged to my father. He used to carry it with him everywhere he went.

> TAMMY
> Why?

> LEON
> He said it gave him good luck...
> (shrugging)
> ...or something like that.

> TAMMY
> (seriously)
> So, why do you carry it?

Leon tilts his head in thought, his demeanor serious as well.

> LEON
> It helps me remember.

> TAMMY
> Remember what?

INT. HALLWAY - DAY - FLASHBACK SEQUENCE (LEON'S MEMORIES)

Leon, 11 years old, sits in a chair outside the MASTER BEDROOM. The door opens. Diego exits. Motions to Leon.

Slowly, Leon stands to his feet. Knees trembling.

INT. MASTER BEDROOM - DAY - FLASHBACK SEQUENCE (LEON'S MEMORIES)

At Peter's bedside stands a frightened Leon. At the other end of the room stands Diego with his hands crossed in front of him.

On the bed rests Peter, plagued by cancer, completely unrecognizable. His face, gaunt and skeletal. Peter struggles to lift his frail hand.

Leon looks down at his father's hand. Inside his palm, the jet.

EXT. PIER - NIGHT - PRESENT DAY

Leon turns his eyes to the brilliant sky, the billions of stars twinkling above. Turns his eyes toward Tammy's.

> TAMMY (O.S.)
> Why hold onto something that makes you sad?

Leon is first to make a move toward Tammy: his hand easing behind Tammy's neck as she readies to embrace his lips.

There, underneath the moonlight, Leon and Tammy share their first kiss.

INT. HALLWAY, HIGH SCHOOL - DAY

As Tammy opens the locker, a folded piece of notebook paper drops heavily to her feet. She picks it up. Opens it. Inside, Leon's jet.

Tammy smiles, eyes brim with tears, holds the jet closely.

INT. LEON'S BEDROOM, LEATHERBY MANOR - NIGHT

Leon is on top of Tammy, making love to her.

As quickly as she can, Tammy removes her shirt, Leon helping her with each button until the shirt is removed.

Next, Leon removes her bra without a hitch. Traces his lips around her neck, then makes his way toward Tammy's breasts.

Leon removes his lips and looks into Tammy's eyes -- Tammy suddenly chokes!

Tammy grabs her throat; Leon pulls away in shock. The bags under his eyes are much darker, the veins around them are more visible; his eyes, pale and sickly.

> LEON
> Tammy! What's wrong?

Tammy sits upright on the bed, her hand around her neck curls and stiffens. Her face goes from purple and blue to the color of ash.

> LEON (CONT'D)
> Diego! Help me! Diego!

Leon helps Tammy to the floor and proceeds to do CPR. Tammy's eyes fixate. Her face falls into a slackened state of horror. She stops choking...

A door swings open from behind!

> DIEGO (O.S.)
> Master Dorsey!

> LEON
> (crying)
> I don't know what happened...we were messing
> around and then she...she started choking...

Diego pushes Leon aside and checks Tammy's pulse. Turns toward Leon. Shocked as well.

INT. LEON'S BEDROOM, LEATHERBY MANOR - DAY

Leon stands behind the same window. Looks below. Diego shakes hands with a TEAM OF MEN dressed in all black, rough-looking, then he looks up at Leon. The strange men get inside a tinted BLACK VAN. They drive off.

INT. COURTYARD, LEATHERBY MANOR - DAY

Leon sits on a bench made of stone, peers at the dark woods surrounding the luxurious estate, LEATHERBY MANOR. Diego approaches from behind.

> DIEGO (O.S.)
> I'm sorry, Master Dorsey. There was nothing they
> could do to save her.

> LEON
> (crying)
> There's something happening to me, Diego...

Leon looks down at his palms, trembling.

> LEON (CONT'D)
> ...I don't know what it is, but I can feel it
> growing inside me. I'm scared...

Diego sighs, sits down on the bench, struggles to make eye contact with Leon.

> DIEGO
> Your father has a friend who lives on an island off
> the coast of India. He's a good man, and he'll
> watch over you for the time being.

> LEON
> (seething)
> Only guilty people run!

> DIEGO
> I'm afraid you don't have any other choice...

With his face reddened, Leon turns to Diego, who, in return, immediately turns away.

> DIEGO (CONT'D)
> (with his head down)
> ...Forgive me, Master Dorsey.

EXT. TARMAC, AIRPORT - DAY

Hesitantly, Leon steps out of the backseat of the car. Grabs the luggage from the trunk.

Diego closes the door behind Leon and walks him to the private jet where the PILOT stands next to the steps, waiting to greet Leon.

INT. AIRPLANE - NIGHT

Leon sits next to the window and watches the last bit of sun fall underneath the blanket of clouds.

EXT. FOOD MARKET - DAY

Downtown Kandy: teeming with Indians and backpackers funneling their way shoulder to shoulder through the narrow corridors between food stands and shops, eyes attached to the cell phones in their hands.

One man in particular stands out among the rest, the most observant one, MARCUS HOPKINS, black, late 30's, Southern accent, well-fit, has a circular white birthmark covering the part of his hair, dressed in a red Hawaiian shirt, Havana hat, khakis, and a pair of mirror-tinted shades.

INT. GARAGE, SURAJ'S AUTO REPAIR - DAY

At least ten taxis fill the garage, all missing parts and ready to be worked on.

A chubby Indian man, SURAJ, 30's, walks over to one taxi in particular.

>   SURAJ
>   (exuberantly)
>   Hey, my main man, Freeze! Time for lunch!

>   LEON (O.S.)
>   (from underneath the taxi)
>   You know I hate it when you call me that.

A grunt from Leon, then the sound of a metallic object striking the ground...

                         SURAJ
          Well, why not?
                    (emphasizing the word *cool*)
          It's a <u>cool</u> name.

                         LEON (O.S.)
          There we go...

While Suraj places his hands over his hips and shifts his weight to one side of his body, Leon, or "Freeze," now 24, puts the final touches on the engine.

He rolls from underneath the engine. Looks up at Suraj who is towering above him. Grease stains in the shape of small continents cover Leon's entire face.

                         LEON (CONT'D)
                    (out of breath)
          ...Have patience, my chubby friend. Lunch will
          always be there.

                         SURAJ
          Lunch will soon be dinner, if you don't stop
          jerking your rod. You work too hard, Freeze.

Suraj grabs the rag from a cart and tosses it at Leon, hitting him in the chest.

                         SURAJ (CONT'D)
          Here. I'm hungry.

Leon places the socket wrench back into the toolbox, grabs the rag. Suraj walks away.

                         LEON
                    (to himself)
          Yeah, Suraj. You're always hungry.

EXT. FOOD MARKET - DAY

A SERVER, a young lady in her late teens, brings Leon and Suraj their food, places it on the table in front of them. Leon looks up at the young lady, smiles.

                         LEON
          Thank you. It smells delicious.

The smitten server "freezes" in her tracks. She stares at Leon with wayward delight. The words escape from her parched mouth, leaving her speechless.

Finally, the server snaps from her daze, moistens her lips, and smiles back. Struts away. Suraj rolls his eyes, then giggles from the server's undeniable attraction to Leon.

> SURAJ
> I don't how you do it, <u>Freeze</u>.

Leon leans closer.

> LEON
> Do you want to know the secret?

> SURAJ
> Of course!

> LEON
> (quietly)
> There is no secret.

Suraj slams his fist on the table.

> SURAJ
> Oh! Come on!

Leon laughs, then draws his attention away from the server walking away. He notices Marcus standing next to a bunch of bananas dangling over a STAND, his attention aimed directly at Leon. Leon stops laughing.

EXT. COFFEE STAND, MARKET - DAY

Leon hands the money to the server, then hands an expresso to Suraj.

> LEON
> Say, Suraj, I'll catch up with you later.

> SURAJ
> No! No! No! We have work to do --

Leon places his hand over Suraj's shoulder.

> LEON
> (jokingly)
> Don't worry. The work will be done by the next
> time you get hungry.

Suraj waves at Leon in disgust, walks away. Then, Leon's demeanor turns stern and unyielding. Directs his attention toward Marcus roaming through the crowds.

EXT. STREET, DOWNTOWN - DAY

Marcus loses Leon as soon as he rounds the intersection. Removes his tinted shades.

In a state of panic, Marcus searches for Leon in the crowds. He turns front to back, left to right; then he finally spots Leon ducking into an alleyway.

Marcus puts on his shades. Follows.

EXT. ALLEYWAY - DAY

As Marcus makes his way past a dumpster, he suddenly stops in his tracks. Peeks over his shoulder.

> LEON (O.S.)
> (from behind)
> Nice shirt.

Marcus turns around, chortles. Leon steps from a corner of the building, partially revealing himself in the shadows.

> MARCUS
> You got me --

> LEON
> Why are you following me?

Leon steps closer, away from the shadows. Marcus holds his hands in the air.

> MARCUS
> Relax, Mr. Dorsey. I've traveled a long way to
> find you --

> LEON
> How do you know my name?

A couple of CIVILIANS exit through the back of a store, startling Leon. They pass both Leon and Marcus standing between the two buildings.

> MARCUS
> Please, Mr. Dorsey. Why don't we continue this
> conversation somewhere else?

Marcus motions across the alley, Leon unsure whether or not to follow.

EXT. ROOFTOP - DAY

Leon reads the business card in his hand; his brows furrow in confusion.

INSERT - THE CARD, which reads:

> "Marcus Hopkins."

BACK TO LEON

who turns to Marcus, now without shades.

> MARCUS
> I work for Aerodyne, a biomedical research
> institution striving to bring new and more
> efficient ways to the field of medicine. We, at
> Aerodyne, feel strongly about acquiring a man of
> your...
> > (thinking)
> ...talents.

> LEON
> My talents? I think you got the wrong guy, pal --

Leon hands the card back to Marcus, who, in return, refuses to take the card.

MARCUS
Please. I have copies.

Marcus takes a step closer to Leon. Dangerously close.

MARCUS (CONT'D)
You know, I can't imagine what it must feel like having to live with the guilt of killing another person, especially the one you loved.

Leon grimaces, doesn't respond.

MARCUS (CONT'D)
What if I were to tell you, Leon, that the organization I work for was capable of wiping your slate clean?

LEON
Sounds too good to be true.

MARCUS
Well, let's just say Aerodyne has a few...
(thinking)
...comfortable benefactors. All you have to do is come back with me to the States where we will conduct a couple of basic tests.

LEON
What kind of tests?

MARCUS
Elementary tests. Basically, we want find out what makes you...
(shrugging)
...you.

Leon turns away from Marcus, walks to the ledge, thinks.

LEON
You want to turn me into a guinea pig. Is that it?

                    MARCUS
    Only if you want us to, Leon. If you do this for
    us, we will provide you with living quarters, a
    job, if you want --

                    LEON
                (to Marcus)
    -- If you are telling the truth, what's in it for me?

                    MARCUS
    A chance.

                    LEON
    A chance for what?

                    MARCUS
    To change the world, of course.

Leon smirks, shakes his head in both amusement and disgust. Marcus walks to
the ledge, moves his peer from the busy streets below to the smoggy Kandy skyline.

                    MARCUS (CONT'D)
    By the time my crew found Ms. Chessman...

EXT. BEACH - DAY - FLASHBACK

A tide washes back toward the sea, revealing a gaping face of stone protruding
from the shore.

                    MARCUS (V.O.)
    ...her body had completely turned to stone.

EXT. ROOFTOP - DAY - PRESENT DAY

Leon rips the business card and crumbles it into the air. Shreds of paper rain
down like tiny white feathers on the street below. He leans away from the ledge.

                    LEON
                (to Marcus)
    Have a safe trip back home, Mr. Hopkins.

Marcus grins. Pulls out the same jet from his pocket. Places it on the ledge.

> MARCUS
> In case you change your mind, I'm staying at the
> Royal Suites, but...
> (coyly)
> ...you already know that.

Leon eyes the jet, then glares at Marcus, who, in return, walks away. Three steps later. Marcus stops, turns his shoulder, puts on his shades.

> MARCUS (CONT'D)
> Every man deserves a second chance. It's your
> choice.

Marcus walks away, again. Stops again. Turns shoulder.

> MARCUS (CONT'D)
> And remember, Leon, you will <u>always</u> have a
> choice.

INT. LEON'S APARTMENT - NIGHT

Leon stands behind an open window, the moon casting its light on the jet between his fingertips; however, it glistens with the same pale light. Not moonlight.

QUICK FLASHES - LEON'S MEMORIES

-- On the pier, Leon leans forward and kisses Tammy for the first time.

-- In his bedroom, Leon suddenly removes his lips from Tammy's lips, now hardening into stone.

Leon directs his attention from the jet to the droves of CIVILIANS walking through the gritty streets.

INT. HOTEL ROOM, ROYAL SUITES - NIGHT

Marcus stands upright in front of the BATHROOM mirror, adjusting his collar, then primping his hair.

A cell phone RINGS from the counter. Marcus picks it up, then answers the call.

INT. LEON'S APARTMENT - CONTINUOUS

Leon stands in front of the window and waits in the pale moonlight.

> LEON
> What guarantees do I have?

> MARCUS (V.O.)
> Full pardon. You have my word.

INT. HOTEL ROOM, ROYAL SUITES - NIGHT

Marcus closes the cell phone; removes the battery from the back and then tosses it in the trash. He opens the top drawer of the nightstand, revealing a HANDGUN. Places Leon's PASSPORT on the nightstand, then grabs the handgun. Turns off the safety. Holsters it.

EXT. ROYAL SUITES - DAY

Marcus exits the hotel, slides a handful of money into the DOORMAN'S hand and meets Leon at the edge of the curb.

> MARCUS
> Are you ready to change the world, Mr. Dorsey?

Leon glances down at the luggage at his feet, takes in a deep breath, then Marcus pats him on the shoulder.

> MARCUS (CONT'D)
> Let's go home. Shall we?

INT. SUV - DAY

Leon rides in the backseat -- his leg rapidly bobbing against the floor -- while Marcus rides in the passenger seat, one of Aerodyne's AGENTS behind the wheel. The ride gets rather bumpy, as they ride along a sketchy highway.

With Leon looking, Marcus secretly reaches into his pocket and pops a pill from a unmarked bottle. Downs it with saliva. Inserts the bottle back into his pocket.

                    LEON
So, tell me how this thing works.

                    MARCUS
Our plane leaves in exactly three hours from
Colombo to Qatar. From Qatar, we'll take Flight
817 to JFK International where my men will be
waiting for our arrival. From there, you go
wherever you tell us to go. Remember, Leon,
you're in control. Not us.

Marcus pulls a passport from his jacket pocket and hands it to Leon.

                    MARCUS (CONT'D)
I almost forgot. You'll be needing this.

Leon looks down at the passport, confused.

                    MARCUS (CONT'D)
I had one of my men 'tweak' it for you. You
shouldn't have any problems getting past Customs.

                    LEON
Shouldn't? I thought you said this thing was a
done deal. Clean slate, remember?

Marcus turns his shoulder, removes his shades, smiles. Leon looks into Marcus's
eyes, something in them, a twinkle...

                    MARCUS
Don't worry, Leon. You're in good hands. If
anything goes wrong, I'll be there every step of --

An engine suddenly REVS!

The SUV jerks forward, then wobbles from side to side, then overturns...

EXT. HIGHWAY - CONTINUOUS

The SUV rolls at least five times before coming to a halt on its roof. The front left side completely smashed like an accordion. Debris scattered along the highway. Eddies of smoke.

The truck that rammed the SUV skids along the fringe of the wreckage. A group of cloaked BANDITS storm from the truck, all carrying assault rifles.

INT. SUV - CONTINUOUS

Hanging upside down, Leon fingers the gash on the side of his forehead. Looks at Marcus, unconscious. The agent, face masked with blood, unconscious as well; however, there doesn't seem to be any life-threatening injuries.

Leon turns to the commotion outside the SUV, sees the bandits advancing toward the SUV. He removes the seat belt, falls to the roof. Slithers toward Marcus. Before he checks his pulse, he finds a gun dangling from his armpit. Grabs it.

EXT. HIGHWAY - CONTINUOUS

The bandits cock their weapons.

> BANDIT
> (in Arabic)
> Make him remember.

A couple of laughs follow.

INT. SUV - CONTINUOUS

Leon slips from the passenger window. Crawls over shattered glass until he frees himself from the SUV.

EXT. HIGHWAY - CONTINUOUS

Leon takes cover behind the SUV. Peeks over the back right tire.

A gunshot suddenly SCREAMS out, the bullet piercing the tread of the tire...

The bandits flank the SUV while Leon seeks cover. Rifles drawn. Leon takes in a deep breath, calms.

Once more, Leon pokes his head from behind the tire, aims the gun, fires a couple of rounds. Hits one of the BANDITS in the arm, forcing him to the ground. Then, he hits two more BANDITS.

The bandits return fire, aggressively, perforating the side of the SUV with bullet holes.

Leon takes cover, then returns fire. No more bullets. He throws the gun aside. Takes cover. Directs his attention inside the SUV, toward Marcus, who is slowly awakening. His natural response: reaching for his gun.

Marcus comes up empty...

One BANDIT approaches from the side, assault rifle aimed at Leon's head. Leon raises his arms in the air, surrenders. The bandit flicks up the barrel of the rifle, motioning for Leon to stand to his feet.

LEON
(out of breath)
What do you want? Money --

Leon stands, slowly, then the butt of a rifle swiftly SMACKS him in the back of the head.

Leon falls to the ground, drifts in and out of consciousness, while the bandits drag a resistant Marcus from the wreckage.

In one last burst of energy, Leon hones in on Marcus. Watches the bandits place Marcus into the back of the truck.

The truck drives away, then we get a CLOSE UP of the license plate: CQ817.

And that's the last thing Leon sees before he passes out, CQ817...

INT. EMERGENCY ROOM - DAY

The sound of rings SLIDING across a metal pole forces Leon from his rest...

Leon's eyes bolt open; he turns toward the curtain, closed; then, he looks underneath the curtain and witnesses the feet of a NURSE walking away. Rolls from the hospital bed, removes the IV from his arm, then grabs hold of a table in order to keep himself from falling after a dizzy spell.

EXT. HOSPITAL - DAY

Looking around in paranoia, Leon slips from the back entrance of the hospital. Reaches in his pocket. Stops. Pulls out his passport. Still intact. Then thinks for a moment.

INT. TAXI - DAY

Leon sits quietly in the backseat and stares at the jet in his hand. The jet glistening faintly.

QUICK FLASHES - LEON'S MEMORIES

-- Leon crawls through the shards of broken glass and catches a glimpse of the licence plate, CQ817.

-- Leon sees the same truck with the same licence plate number, CQ817, parked outside his apartment while he grabs groceries from the FOOD MARKET.

EXT. CAFE - DAY - FLASHBACK SEQUENCE (LEON'S MEMORIES)

Leon, 22 years old, exits with Suraj, only to be swarmed by a CROWD of pedestrians (most of them are walking automatically on the busy sidewalks, talking on cell phones).

> SURAJ
> (laughing)
> So, I ask her: What's the difference between a
> man and a monkey? She shrugs and says, 'What?'
> So, I pull down my pants and --

A STRANGE MAN with a jagged scar running down the side of his face suddenly cuts through Leon and Suraj, bumping shoulders with both of them. Suraj turns to the strange man.

SURAJ (CONT'D)
Yeah! Watch where you're going!

Leon carefully watches the strange man walk to the same truck. He gets inside the truck. Drives off.

INT. GARAGE - DAY - FLASHBACK SEQUENCE (LEON'S MEMORIES)

Peter's friend, TOMAS, 60's, introduces a pale and timid Leon, 19 years old, to an animated Indian man named Suraj.

TOMAS
This is Suraj.

Suraj tosses an oily rag over his shoulder. Holds out his hand. Leon shakes his hand.

TOMAS (CONT'D)
Don't worry, Leon. You're in good hands...

INT. SUV - DAY - FLASHBACK SEQUENCE (LEON'S MEMORIES)

Marcus turns his shoulder, looks into Leon's eyes.

MARCUS
Don't worry, Leon. You're in good hands.

INT. BEDROOM, HIDEOUT - DAY - PRESENT DAY

Marcus's hands are tied behind an old chair positioned in the middle of a dingy BEDROOM overlooking the MARKET in DOWNTOWN KANDY.

One side of Marcus's face is covered with blood, the other half covered with fresh bruises.

A phantom of a smirk creeps onto Marcus's face. He carries that look in his eye, a twinkle...

INT. TAXI - DAY - PRESENT DAY

Leon inserts the jet back into his pocket.

> LEON
> (to driver)
> Take me back to Kandy --

The TAXI DRIVER points ahead, frustrated.

> TAXI DRIVER
> But, sir, we're only a couple of miles away --

Leon stares directly at the taxi driver's eyes in the rear view mirror. They share a long stare, then the taxi driver wipes the sweat from his brow, then clears his throat.

> TAXI DRIVER (CONT'D)
> (voice trembling)
> Yes, sir.

EXT. STREET, DOWNTOWN KANDY - DAY

Leon steps out of the taxi, pays the driver, and stands before his APARTMENT building. Looks around the crowded streets. The same truck, Leon sees, parked across the street.

INT. HALLWAY, APARTMENT COMPLEX - DAY

As Leon sticks his head from the corner of the wall, he finds two BANDITS guarding a door at the end of the hallway. He ducks back behind the wall. Thinks for a moment.

Leon's attention is drawn to three CIVILIANS -- in their 20's -- playing on the sidewalk. One of them shoves the other.

> CIVILIAN #1
> Quit playing!

Leon's eyes drift into thought.

We CUT TO the three CIVILIANS strolling down the hallway. One of them looks different, head down -- elusive -- while the other two remain disruptive.

> CIVILIAN #1 (CONT'D)
> Did you see the Los Angeles Lakers crush the
> 76ers last night? Shaquille O'Neal is the man!

CIVILIAN #2
Hey! They don't call him the 'Shaq' for nothing.

The bandits, armed with assault rifles, acknowledge the commotion and step from their posts.

BANDIT
(approaching the civilians)
This is a restricted area.

CIVILIAN #1
Restricted area? Says who?

The THIRD civilian -- the elusive one -- finally raises his head. Slowly. Removes the baseball cap...

Both bandits' eyes swell from the sight of the civilian's face, Leon's face!

LEON
(whispering)
Get down...

Leon squeezes through the two civilians, pushes them to the floor, and takes out the first BANDIT: first, Leon shoves the rifle away and grabs the bandit's head and slams it against the wall, knocking him unconscious!

Then, the second BANDIT aims at Leon from behind. Leon ducks out of the way as the bandit fires. Leon grabs the end of the rifle, now twirling around in circles while the bandit continues to fire. Bullets swirl all around like a cyclone.

Once the clip empties, Leon rams the butt of the rifle into the bandit's chin, forcing the bandit backwards. Leon punches his abdomen, which is left exposed.

The bandit lurches forward, swings at Leon, but Leon dodges; and in his counterattack -- while using his entire body -- he throws a hammer of a blow across the bandit's face. Leon falls to the floor. So too does the unconscious bandit.

Rising from his kneeled stance, Leon turns his shoulder to the civilians, both unharmed.

The speechless civilians stare at Leon with vacant expressions. They tense up, both of them. Then scurry away.

INT. APARTMENT - DAY

Leon opens the door, steps inside, only to find a fairly empty LIVING ROOM.

INT. LIVING ROOM - CONTINUOUS

Positioned in the middle of the room is a raggedy couch that looks as if it spent most of its days on the side of the street. Several used bottles of water are scattered throughout the room. There's a radio on the KITCHEN counter, which is playing a SOCCER game on a whisper-like volume.

Leon closes the door behind him. Carefully.

We hear a sudden CREAK, but it's not coming from the door!

Leon directs his attention toward the BATHROOM, then a lanky SHADOW sliding across the walls. He approaches the bathroom. Arrives.

As Leon cracks open the door, another BANDIT carrying a KNIFE pounces from a dimly lit BEDROOM. Leon dodges the path of the knife, tosses the bandit through the door.

INT. BATHROOM - CONTINUOUS

Both Leon and the bandit wrestle around the tight space. Punches are thrown in short bursts, Leon mostly using his elbows to fend off each jab of the knife.

The bandit manages to catch the side of Leon's arm with the blade.

Leon retaliates, BANGS the bandit's hand against the sink several times until the sink is smashed to bits. The knife falls from the bandit's hand. However, the bandit lands a left hook, forcing Leon into the mirror. Glass shatters.

Quickly, Leon grabs a SHARD of glass. Swipes. The bandit ducks, the sharp glass missing his face by inches.

The bandit, now weaponless, swings once more at Leon. Knocks the shard of glass from Leon's hand, sending it across the bathroom.

Leon grabs a hand towel from the floor and rolls out of the way from another punch. Leaps onto the toilet and wraps the towel around the bandit's throat.

They struggle, both Leon and the bandit. They end up crashing through the thin wall.

INT. GUEST BEDROOM - CONTINUOUS

Leon takes the better end of the fall.

Now towering over the bandit, Leon keeps the pressure applied to the bandit's throat until he chokes him out.

As Leon releases the towel and catches his breath, another BANDIT carrying a knife pounces from behind. Leon rolls out of the way. Grabs the shard of glass from earlier and cuts the bandit's Achilles heel while in his down stroke.

The bandit collapses, screaming bloody horror. Leon pins the bandit's shoulders to the floor, presses the glass to his throat. The bandit looks into Leon's eyes.

Subtly, the bandit shakes his head no.

Leon tilts his head in bafflement. Peers into the bandit's eyes. Something strange in them, his eyes...

INT. BEDROOM - DAY

With the bandit's handgun in hand, Leon kicks open the door, only to find yet another BANDIT standing at one end of the room while Marcus sitting at the other.

While keeping the gun aimed at the bandit, Leon inspects Marcus's injuries, the blood on his swollen face, his hands tied, weakened posture.

The bandit cocks the hammer of the pistol, aims it at Marcus's head.

> BANDIT
> Drop the gun or your friend dies. Your choice...

Leon wipes the string of blood from the side of his face, keeps the gun on the bandit.

                    LEON
                (out of breath)
            He's not my friend.

                    MARCUS
        Shoot the son of a bitch! He'll kill us both!

Leon thinks, then tosses the gun on the floor. Obediently places his hands in the
air.

                    LEON
            What do you want?

                    BANDIT
        Since your friend here no longer has any
        importance to us, you're going to watch him die.

                    LEON
        I told you, 'He's not my friend.'

The sides of Leon's face flex like tiny fists. Nostrils flare.

The bandit cocks the pistol. Aims at Marcus. Marcus closes his eyes. And keeps
them closed.

Leon's pale face QUAKES, slowly at first and then violently. His eyes narrow as
he turns them toward the bandit, who, in return, spots Leon in the corner of his
eye.

The bandit's hand starts to tremble, violently. The pistol slips from his grip as his
eyes lock with Leon's now white eyes.

A trail of blood trickles from the bandit's right nostril.

                    BANDIT
            What are you doing? Stop. Please...

Beads of sweat build all around Leon's forehead, his honed eyes never leaving the
bandit's eyes.

The bandit falls to his knees, grabs the side of his forehead in incredible agony.
Screaming bloody horror...

Meanwhile, Leon's eyes swell in a maddening rage. The veins around them darkening as well. Wind gusts around his head. Each strand of hair moving in the air like snakes.

The blood streams from the bandit's nose; his head shakes too, as he convulses on the floor and dies.

Leon gasps, then coughs, then gags, then, finally, catches his breath.

The force he exerted causes his posture to weaken as well. Falls to one knee, trying to shake away the dizzy spell. Looks down at his hand, shaking as fast as the rattle of a snake. Focuses. Then, the shaking eventually stops.

Leon stands, carefully. Walks over to Marcus, who carefully cracks open his eyes. Leon unties his bound hands from behind the chair.

> LEON
> Can you walk?

Marcus stretches his jaw, grimaces, then stands.

> MARCUS
> I'll live.

Now intrigued, Marcus walks across the room. Stands over the bloody corpse. Still left in awe.

> MARCUS (CONT'D)
> How did you do that?

No response from Leon.

> MARCUS (CONT'D)
> He didn't turn. Why?

Leon walks to the window. Doesn't respond. Instead, he looks outside at the busy streets. At innocent people.

> MARCUS (O.S.) (CONT'D)
> We can train you. You know. We can show you
> how to control this gift of yours.

No response, again.

> MARCUS (CONT'D)
> How many more people have to die before you
> realize who you really are?

Leon turns his shoulder, faces Marcus.

> LEON
> It's not a gift.

> MARCUS
> Then, what is it?

> LEON
> It's a curse.

> MARCUS
> (seriously)
> Maybe so, but it doesn't have to be that way.

INT. SUV - NIGHT

Both Leon and Marcus ride in the backseat while the AGENT -- different one --
pulls through a gated area outside an AIRPORT. Marcus turns to Leon. Notices
his quiet state.

> MARCUS
> The man you killed was Abdul Hawsawi. Before
> I arrived in Sri Lanka, my men informed me
> about Hawsawi and his crew.

> LEON
> What did they want from you?

> MARCUS
> Not me, Leon.

Leon doesn't respond, already knows the answer.

> MARCUS (CONT'D)
> If people like Hawsawi can find you, then it's
> only a matter of time before someone far more
> dangerous finds you.

Leon's eyes drift in thought. Sighs.

> MARCUS (CONT'D)
> Did you get a good look at the taxi driver?

INT. TAXI - DAY - FLASHBACK SEQUENCE (LEON'S MEMORIES)

Leon looks into the rear view mirror, notices the bead of sweat crawling down the side of the taxi driver's temple.

INT. GUEST BEDROOM - DAY - FLASHBACK SEQUENCE (LEON'S MEMORIES)

Leon looms over the unconscious bandit before him. Gets a closer look at his face, which turns out being the taxi driver's face...

INT. SUV - NIGHT - PRESENT DAY

Still baffled, Leon turns to Marcus.

> LEON
> (trailing off)
> I don't understand. I was on my way to Colombo
> --

> MARCUS
> -- where a handful of Hawsawi's men were
> waiting for you. Hawsawi's plan was to make it
> look as if they were kidnapping me, when, in
> fact, they were only kidnapping you. Can't lure a
> fish without a bait.

A soft SQUEAK of brakes. The SUV stops.

> AGENT (O.S.)
> We're here.

EXT. TERMINAL - CONTINUOUS

The agent parks the SUV in front of a secluded airplane HANGER. A couple of Gulfstream V's parked inside. A TEAM OF AGENTS -- over a dozen -- surround the planes.

INT. SUV - CONTINUOUS

Leon stares out the window. Reflects.

> MARCUS (O.S.)
> After Aerodyne found out about what happened,
> they sent us a little present. Beats flying coach.

A tense silence. Leon turns away from the window. Looks into Marcus's eyes.

INT. HANGER - NIGHT

As Marcus and Leon walk toward the GV, Marcus nods at the AGENTS from Aerodyne's security team. Ends up shaking hands with one of the agents, who turns out being the same scarred-face BANDIT from before. During the handshake, a device is exchanged; however, we don't see the device.

EXT. LANDING STRIP - DAY

The GV lands on a desolate landing strip outside Bangor, Maine. Parks.

Both Marcus and Leon step from the plane onto the ground where a black SUV waits for them.

Standing outside the SUV are two individuals: one is a CHAUFFEUR, a nameless android, casual clothes, parted blonde hair, vacant expression; and then other is STAFF, 30's, bomber jacket, dark hair, rough-looking, armed to the gills.

EXT. LEATHERBY MANOR - DAY

A typical overcast day in northern Maine. The rain is cool and misty.

Leon wipes the sweat from his hands over his pants as he stands underneath an overhang.

The heavy door SWINGS open, revealing Diego, now in his early 50's; however, he still looks remarkably fit for his age.

> DIEGO
> (surprised)
> Master Dorsey?

> LEON
> Long time...

Diego steps forward, smiles, then hugs Leon.

> DIEGO
> Too long.

Leon pulls himself from Diego, turns his shoulder, shoots a glance at the black SUV parked in the driveway.

> DIEGO (CONT'D)
> Friends of yours, sir?

> LEON
> Come, Diego...
> (patting Diego's shoulder)
> ...We have a lot of catching up to do.

Before Diego walks back inside, he directs his attention toward the SUV. Then glares.

INT. EAST WING, LEATHERBY MANOR - DAY

Diego walks alongside Leon, occasionally pointing at the walls and furniture which make up the GREAT ROOM.

> DIEGO
> As you can see, I left everything the way it was
> when you left, sir.

They come across a bust of MARCUS AURELIUS perched on a mount where a grandfather clock once stood.

>   DIEGO (CONT'D)
>   Well...
>   (trailing off)
>   ...not everything.

INT. GALLERY, LEATHERBY MANOR - DAY

Leon strolls around the gutted room. All of the artifacts, gone. The ancient paintings and sculptures, gone as well. The Medusa head, gone.

Perplexed from the emptiness of the room, Leon turns toward Diego, who is standing at the doorway.

>   LEON
>   Where did it all go?

>   DIEGO
>   I moved your father's belongings underground, sir.

Leon shakes his head, furrows his brows.

>   LEON
>   Why?

>   DIEGO
>   Let's just say -- after you left, Master Dorsey --
>   things got a bit 'hectic' around here.

INT. THE BUNKER - DAY

The door opens, kicking up clouds of dust. Two silhouettes stand inside the lit doorway. Peering downward. A sword of light slices through all the dust, as well as the bloated belly of darkness below.

Both Diego and Leon walk down the steep staircase, Diego leading the way.

                    DIEGO
Your father devoted his entire life into trying to
understand the origins of mankind. He even
sacrificed the one thing every man holds dear to
his heart...

They both arrive at the base of the stairs, stop. Diego squares himself to Leon,
looks into his eyes.

                    DIEGO (CONT'D)
...fatherhood.

Leon turns away. Looks around the darkness.

                    DIEGO (CONT'D)
Your father loved you. More than you'll ever
know.

                    LEON
          (to Diego)
Where is she?

Diego turns around, flicks on a flashlight, then guides Leon to Medusa's head.
Leon approaches the glass case while Diego turns on the light bulb overhead.

The light shines upon an EMPTY case. No Medusa head.

                    DIEGO
Forgive me, Master Dorsey. The years I spent
paying off lawyers took a substantial toll on your
father's inheritance.

Leon stands before the empty case. Grimaces.

                    DIEGO (CONT'D)
They promised me security. So, I made a deal
with them...

                    LEON
          (quietly)
You had no right.

Diego approaches. Leon faces Diego. Still angry.

> DIEGO
> One day, you will have to make a sacrifice as I
> did, as well as your father. Let's just hope, Master
> Dorsey, history doesn't repeat itself.

INT./EXT. SUV - DAY

Marcus sees Leon approaching. Steps out. Opens the door for Leon.

As Leon enters the SUV, Marcus DROPS his cell phone. The sudden SMACK
on the ground grabs Leon's attention. Leon shakes his head in annoyance.

Marcus kneels down; and as he picks up the phone, he places the same
MYSTERIOUS device underneath the well of the rear right tire without anyone
paying attention. Pockets the cell phone. Then nods at Leon. Gets back inside
the SUV.

EXT. PIER - DAY

As the last bit of sun struggles to break through the newspaper gray skies above --
parts of the sun glistening off the Atlantic Ocean -- Leon looks down at the jet in
his hand.

He shakes away the memory. Tosses the jet into the ocean.

EXT. DEATH VALLEY - DAY

From above, we see the same black SUV speeding down a narrow dirt road
splitting through a small, lifeless VALLEY.

The SUV arrives at a secured gate where THREE GUARDS with assault rifles
perch outside. Heavily armed. Two guards flank the vehicle, one at the driver's
side and the other at the passenger's, while the third one runs a WAND
underneath the car, checking for any mysterious devices, including bombs or even
tracking devices.

The guard waves the detector underneath the back right of the SUV. Nothing. The guard pauses for a moment, then proceeds to check the rest of the SUV.

> GUARD
> (to the other guards)
> It's clean.

The other guard places a SCANNER in front of the chauffeur's eye. A tiny RED LIGHT, as fine as wire, slides across its eye, highlighting the gears and mechanics which make up the artificial eye.

On the scanner, the light flashes GREEN, then reads, "CLEAR."

The guard peeks inside the SUV and witnesses both Leon and Marcus seated in the backseat, both of their faces cloaked with BLACK BAGS.

EXT. MAIN STREET - DAY

The sign perched outside the ghost town reads, "WELCOME TO EDEN."

The SUV drives down a vacant street with local Mom and Pop shops lining the entire strip, all deserted. The only life comes from a merry piece of NEWSPAPER skipping along the sidewalk like tumbleweed.

EXT. BOB'S HARDWARE - CONTINUOUS

The SUV parks in front of a local hardware store. Both the chauffeur and Staff step from the vehicle.

INT. SUV - CONTINUOUS

Staff pulls out two AMMONIA INHALANTS from the glove compartment. Cracks open both of them. Places one underneath Leon's nose, then another underneath Marcus's nose. Both wake with a sudden flinch!

EXT./INT. BOB'S HARDWARE - CONTINUOUS

Both Marcus and Leon, still wearing bags over their heads, are escorted into the dusty store. The door opens with a DING of a cowbell...

The bags are removed from their heads -- both men in a state of disorientation. They look around the store. Empty. Then, Leon turns to Marcus, who is clearing the blur from his eyes with the palm of his hand.

> LEON
> (confusedly)
> You too?

Marcus shakes off the drowsiness. Sighs.

> MARCUS
> Aerodyne is extremely particular about keeping their whereabouts unknown.

> LEON
> (looking around)
> Where are we?

> STAFF
> This way, gentlemen.

Staff pulls upward on the handle of a trowel hanging on the wall of tools. The walls split apart and open, revealing an elevator behind what used to be a wall. Presses the only button, the DOWN ARROW.

The elevator doors open; and once more, Leon and Marcus look at each other. Leon, confused. Marcus, not so much.

INT. ELEVATOR - DAY

Leon, Marcus, and Staff ride in the elevator toward the bottom floor. Leon glances at Marcus's hand. Notices Marcus wiping the sweat along his pant leg. Then watches each floor count down until the elevator reaches LEVEL 1. Doors open.

> STAFF
> Welcome to Aerodyne.

He points ahead.

> STAFF (CONT'D)
> Right this way.

Leon is first to step from the elevator.

INT. HALLWAY, AERODYNE - CONTINUOUS

A narrow hallway -- covered in whiteness -- stretches as far as the eye can see. A strange and yet subtle hum, Leon notices, coming from the walls.

> LEON
> (to Staff)
> What's that noise?

> PASSENGER
> This entire underground facility runs off geothermal energy. Please, Mr. Dorsey, save your questions for Mr. Zappin.

Staff points ahead, again.

INT. LEON'S SUITE, AERODYNE - DAY

Staff opens the door for Leon. All three, including Marcus, walk through the FOYER and into the LIVING ROOM -- Leon mostly admiring the opulence all around, the high-end furniture, as well as other accessories made from glass, including the television, which looks like a piece of glass mounted against the wall.

The living room window, which covers the entire wall, displays a panoramic image of an ocean-front view.

> LEON
> (to Staff)
> I thought you said this place was underground?

A resonant voice from the DINING ROOM.

> VOICE (O.S.)
> Don't let the view fool you, Mr. Dorsey...

Leon turns to the voice, the footsteps of wing tip shoes coming from behind the corner of the wall.

A MAN in his late 30's reveals himself: DAVID ZAPPIN, birth name, David Barros, adopted son of Joseph Zappin, slender and handsome, dark gelled hair, dark eyes, dressed in Johnny Cash-black. He points to the projection of the ocean.

> DAVID
> ...What do you think?

Leon doesn't respond, too overwhelmed with the luxurious suite; then David nods at Staff.

> DAVID (CONT'D)
> I'm sure it's a lot to take in right now...
> (nodding at Staff)
> ...Do you mind giving us the room?

> STAFF
> Yes, sir.

Staff follows suit. Nods at Marcus, then they exit. David smiles, walks toward Leon, extends hand.

> DAVID
> David Zappin. Pleasure to finally meet you in the flesh.

> LEON
> I guess you're the one I have to thank for all of this.

> DAVID
> How was the ride? Not too bumpy, I hope.

> LEON
> (looking around)
> Except for not remembering a single thing as to how I got here, it was fine.

David picks up the remote from the counter.

> DAVID
> Right. My apologies. When you possess one of the greatest discoveries known to man, you have to be extremely...

He pauses for a moment, thinking of the right word to use.

                    DAVID (CONT'D)
...<u>Cautious</u>.
                    (nodding at the window)
          I can change the view, if you like.

Leon doesn't respond. David aims the remote at the window and hits a button.
The window displays a skyline of Downtown Kandy.

                    LEON
          What is this place?

David squints his eyes, suspicious.

                    DAVID
          Hopefully, we plan to make it your new home,
          Mr. Dorsey.

A sigh from David. He places the remote back on the counter.

                    LEON
          You're the one who can wipe my slate clean?

David laughs, slaps Leon on the shoulder. Walks over to the sofa table where he
pours Leon, as well as himself, a glass of scotch.

                    DAVID
          Like father like son. My father used to tell me
          stories about Peter. All work and no play...
                    (shaking his head)
          ...I admire a man who skips the foreplay and gets
          right down to business.

                    LEON
          How did you know my father?

David walks toward Leon. Hands him the drink.

                    LEON (CONT'D)
          I don't drink.

                    DAVID
                    (quietly)
          Very well...

David places the drink on the glass coffee table.

DAVID (CONT'D)
I didn't know your father -- personally -- but my
father did...
            (facing Leon)
...They used to work together. And if I can
convince you to join Aerodyne, so can we.

Leon's eyes fall onto a blown up black and white photograph of the WRIGHT
BROTHERS on the wall.

DAVID (CONT'D)
Ah! The Wright brothers.

David walks to the framed photograph. Drink in hand. Points.

LEON
            (studying photograph)
The first flight at Kill Devil Hills.

DAVID
You know your history.

Leon shrugs, then frowns.

LEON
A little.

DAVID
            (in deep thought)
I can't possibly imagine what Wilbur Wright was
thinking when he witnessed his brother, Orville,
take to the sky for the first time. This country
needs more people like the Wright brothers:
innovators, visionaries...

David turns around, faces Leon. Grins strangely.

DAVID (CONT'D)
...risk takers.

INT. CONTAINMENT ROOM, AERODYNE - DAY

A TEAM OF SCIENTISTS is revealed behind a secured pane of glass holding
Medusa's head. Surrounding the head remains a tall rock face of jet -- the glow
from the jet highlighting each crack and blemish of Medusa's scaly, withered skin.

> DAVID (V.O.)
> The last remnants of the Old World in the palms
> of our hands.

David turns to Leon, studies his vacant facial gesture.

> DAVID (CONT'D)
> Tell me, Mr. Dorsey. What would you do if you
> held the power of a god in your hands?

> LEON
> Maybe you should've studied up on your Greek
> mythology, Mr. Zappin. She was a mortal...
> > (shaking his head)
> ...<u>Not</u> a god.

No response from David. He pats Leon on the back. Guides him down the
hallway.

INT. GALLERY, LEATHERBY MANOR - DAY - FLASHBACK SEQUENCE

Peter carefully places Medusa's head inside a glass case.

> DAVID (V.O.)
> Knowing the way both of our fathers felt about
> 'preserving' history --

EXT. SINKHOLE - DAY - FLASHBACK SEQUENCE

Joseph, much younger, uses the chisel and chips away the rare jet stone from the
cave which houses the head of Medusa. Holds it close to his face.

> DAVID (V.O.)
> -- as you already know -- they felt as if their
> discovery was best kept a secret. My father,
> especially.

INT. CONTAINMENT ROOM, AERODYNE - DAY - PRESENT DAY

David and Leon walk through the laboratories surrounding Medusa's head, David leading the way.

> DAVID
> I'm honoring not only my father's wishes, but also your father's. We're soon going to be living in an age where nothing is kept secret.

Leon turns his attention toward a door at the end of the hallway. Heavily guarded.

INT. HALLWAY, AERODYNE - DAY

With his hands in his pocket, David walks with Leon. Both casual in manner.

> DAVID
> When my father was doing research on Medusa, he concluded that this rare mineraloid called jet gave off an iridescent light whenever it was near the head.

INT. CONTAINMENT ROOM, AERODYNE - DAY

David nods at a chunk of jet on a table. Not glowing.

> DAVID
> We've tested the head with other jets found in various locations of the world...
> (shaking his head)
> ...The other jet doesn't glow. Not like this.

INT. QUARANTINE, AERODYNE - DAY - FLASHBACK SEQUENCE

Day One.

We only see the hand of a SCIENTIST injecting a needle containing a BLACK SERUM into the butt of a MOUSE.

> DAVID (V.O.)
> Over years of research, my father found that the
> jet produced medicinal benefits. He was able to
> synthesize the residue from the jet.

The mouse suddenly rejects the serum, seizures, then stiffens like a board.

> DAVID (V.O.) (CONT'D)
> Numerous times, my father failed; however,
> where there is progress, there is sacrifice.

Week Four.

Another injection, but this time into a paraplegic mouse.

> DAVID (V.O.) (CONT'D)
> Subject 453 proved significant results. It was the
> first breakthrough. Before the injection, the
> lower half of Subject 453 was paralyzed.

INT. HALLWAY, AERODYNE - DAY - PRESENT DAY

Leon turns to David. They both stop.

> LEON
> Paralyzed?

> DAVID
> That's right. After the injections, Subject 453
> could walk. However...

INT. BEDROOM, AERODYNE - DAY - FLASHBACK SEQUENCE

A SCIENTIST walks into the room, only to find SUBJECT 453 contorted and mutilated in a cage. Twisted like a pretzel.

> DAVID (V.O.)
> ...three days later, Subject 453 died. The jet was
> proven to be extremely volatile.

INT. LABORATORY, AERODYNE - NIGHT - FLASHBACK SEQUENCE

In SLOW MOTION, the scientist rages, throwing around things, including important test tubes and whatnot. Destruction.

> DAVID (V.O.)
> The project was later scraped.

INT. COURTYARD, AERODYNE - DAY - PRESENT DAY

David walks Leon through a marbled pathway surrounded by a lush spring landscape of trees and brilliant flowers, all digitalized on a jumbo screen (similar to the projection of the ocean in Leon's suite).

> LEON
> Was my father involved in these experiments?

> DAVID
> From what I was told, your father was more of
> the adventurous type.

> LEON
> All of this sounds interesting, but what the hell
> does it have to do with me?

> DAVID
> Before my grandfather passed away, he told me,
> 'Throughout the world lies a secret gem waiting to
> be discovered. And it is our job to find it.'

They stop walking. Face each other.

> DAVID (CONT'D)
> I believe you, Leon, are that secret gem.

INT. HOSPITAL ROOM, SAINT GABRIEL - CONTINUOUS

Joseph rests in a hospital bed with a breathing tube attached to his neck.

> DAVID (V.O.)
> Last year, my father was involved in a skiing
> accident which left him paralyzed.

INT. OBSERVATIONAL ROOM E, AERODYNE - DAY

Both David and Leon stand behind a mirror. On the other side of the mirror is a RECREATIONAL ROOM where Joseph sits in a wheelchair in front of a window. Stares out with a vacant expression. A TEAM OF THERAPISTS stand around him.

> DAVID
> What my father failed to realize was that the cure didn't lie inside the jet...
> > (to Leon)
> ...I believe what you hold inside you can not only save my father's life, but also save the lives of millions.

INT. HALLWAY, AERODYNE - DAY

David exits Leon's suite; finds Marcus standing against the wall.

> DAVID
> So, Mr. Hopkins, how did it go between you and Hawsawi?

> MARCUS
> You don't have to worry about him anymore.

Marcus reaches in his pocket, pulls out a USB flash drive, and hands it to David.

> MARCUS (CONT'D)
> I captured it all on video.

> DAVID
> Good. One less employee I have to worry about.

David pockets the drives, grins.

> DAVID (CONT'D)
> Well, it seems Leon has proven himself to be more loyal than I thought...
> > (leaning closer)
> **(MORE)**

                    DAVID (CONT'D)
...You see, Mr. Hopkins, loyalty can be a greater
commodity than food or water; and it will get
you extremely far in this business.

David winks at Marcus, then pats him on the shoulder.

                    DAVID (CONT'D)
          Remember that.

Marcus nods with a vacant facial expression.

                    DAVID (CONT'D)
                (walking away)
          Why don't you stick around for a day or two? I
          could use a man of your expertise.

                    MARCUS
                (mumbling)
          Sure thing.

INT. LEON'S SUITE, AERODYNE - NIGHT

Leon stares at the Wright brothers photograph on the wall. Sips from a glass of
aged scotch. Grimaces from the scotch's bite. Places the glass on the table.

INT. TESTING ROOM A, AERODYNE - DAY

Hooked up to monitors, Leon anxiously sits in a chair. The room is bare, except
for the monitors, as well as the screen hanging before Leon. The walls are made
on solid concrete. The atmosphere, cold and drab.

Placing the final plug on Leon's forehead is DOCTOR MONAGHAN, or "Bee,"
which stands for Briana, early 40's, red hair, narrow face, attractive and yet stern,
one of a handful of doctors and scientists in the room. The rest of the team...

INT. OBSERVATIONAL ROOM A, AERODYNE - CONTINUOUS

...remains here, behind a tinted pane of glass. The rest of the team mostly
consists of suits and ties -- David and Marcus being among them -- then
ATTORNEYS.

INT. TESTING ROOM, AERODYNE - CONTINUOUS

Bee finishes taking Leon's blood pressure. Removes the cuff. Then writes Leon's blood pressure on a clipboard.

>   BEE
>   Relax, Mr. Dorsey. There's nothing to be worried
>   about.

>   LEON
>   What's all of this for?

>   BEE
>   We want to know what's going on inside that
>   head of yours.

Bee sits down in a chair next to Leon, crosses her legs.

>   BEE (CONT'D)
>   (closely)
>   I am going to show you a series of random images
>   on the screen behind me and I want you to tell
>   me the first word that comes to mind when you
>   see the image. For example, if I was to be shown
>   an image of the Holocaust, I would say, 'tragedy.'
>   A picture of a shark, 'predator.' Or an ocean --

>   LEON
>   (interrupting)
>   -- Beautiful.

Bee blushes, bats her eyelids. Turns away.

>   BEE
>   You get the idea.

Leon directs his attention toward the wide mirror on the wall.

>   BEE (O.S.) (CONT'D)
>   All right. Let's begin.

The lights dim. The projector SWITCHES on, casting a light over Leon's eyes. The first image is displayed on the screen: a photograph of a baby sleeping in a crib.

BEE (O.S.) (CONT'D)
What's the first word that comes to mind?

LEON
New beginnings.

BEE
Please. Just one word, Mr. Dorsey.

LEON
(sighing)
Hope.

Bee changes the next slide in the projector. Second image: a premature baby inside an incubator.

BEE
Now this. One word.

LEON
(thinking)
Fragile.

The slide changes. Third image: a snake waiting inside a dark hole, its eyes as sharp as sabers.

LEON (CONT'D)
Patience.

Slide changes. Fourth image: same snake, but this time leaping in the air with its fangs clapped down on a dead field mouse. Leon clears his throat.

The needle on the chart next to him spikes a little, then settles.

LEON (CONT'D)
Survival.

Fifth image: the historic "NAPALM GIRL" photograph taken after a bombing in South Vietnam.

Leon cringes from the horrific image. The needle spikes more so than before.

BEE
Mr. Dorsey?

> LEON
> Irreversible.

Sixth image: a dead man lying on a set of train tracks, half of his intestines spilled over the ground.

> LEON (CONT'D)
> Consequences.

ON THE MONITOR

Leon's heart rate jumps from 80 bpm to 120 bpm and continues to rise.

The seventh image: a woman in a hospital, legs spread open, giving birth to a baby.

> BEE
> One word, Mr. Dorsey.

Leon clears his throat, doesn't answer. Sweat beads form around his forehead. His breath, now labored.

> LEON
> (quietly)
> Stop.

Bee studies the readings on the chart, as well as Leon's vitals. Yet, she continues to change the slides.

The IMAGES become more violent now, mostly centered around death, sex, or murder -- even rapidly changing before Leon has a chance to respond; and when Leon responds, his only word is STOP.

The last image: a courtyard statue of a young girl.

> LEON (CONT'D)
> (furiously)
> I said, 'STOP!' GODDAMN IT!

The needle suddenly breaks in half, ink splattering over the graph paper...

Leon rips off the plugs from his body and exits the room.

> LEON (CONT'D)
> We're done here.

INT. OBSERVATIONAL ROOM A, AERODYNE - CONTINUOUS

David rotates around and glares at Marcus, who stands in the back of the room.

> DAVID
> (nodding)
> You're up.

INT. HALLWAY, AERODYNE - CONTINUOUS

Leon storms away, angrier than hell.

> MARCUS (O.S.)
> Leon! Wait a second!

Marcus catches up to Leon, tries to keep pace.

> MARCUS (CONT'D)
> Leon...

Marcus grabs Leon by the arm; then, Leon stops and rotates around, slowly moving his eyes from the floor to Marcus's eyes.

They're much different now, Leon's eyes: the pupil is almost white, not black; and the iris, once an ocean blue, now pale and murky.

Observing the strangeness in Leon's eyes, Marcus lets go of Leon's arm. Cautiously. Takes a step back. Keeps his eyes away from Leon's.

> MARCUS (CONT'D)
> (carefully)
> Relax, Leon. I'm on your side.

> LEON
> (seething)
> I know what you people are trying to do to me...

                    MARCUS
        I never said it was going to be easy, Leon. I
        know you still feel guilty about what --

                    LEON
        -- Don't.

                    MARCUS
        What if I told you there was a way you could
        reverse what was done?

INT. STORAGE ROOM, AERODYNE - DAY

The only light: canned lights suspended from the rafters above, casting rings of
light upon the pavement below. Marcus walks Leon through a ring of light in the
middle of aisles stocked with large pallets of supplies. A line of forklifts is being
charged next to a battery station.

They both walk to the end of one aisle in particular, Marcus leading the way.
Another light switches on...

In front of them is a statue of Tammy Chessman, still 17 years old, still remaining
the same way Leon last saw her, gaping expression, hands clutching her throat;
however, Tammy's perched upright.

                    LEON
                (breathing heavily)
        Why are you showing me this?

Leon walks closer, gets a better look, while Marcus keeps his distance.

                    MARCUS
        They think that your gaze also has the ability to
        undo what it has already done.

                    LEON
        Gaze?

> MARCUS
> That's what they're calling it. Fire and ice, Leon.
> You may think it's a curse. But they're convinced
> it's a gift. You still have a chance to save her --

Leon's eyes water. He grimaces. Holds in the tears.

> LEON
> It won't work.

> MARCUS
> And what makes you so sure?

> LEON
> Because I've already tried. My first night in
> Kandy...

EXT. ALLEYWAY, DOWNTOWN KANDY - NIGHT - FLASHBACK

Crying, Leon sits against the wall. Next to him a stray CAT, scraggly and malnourished, meows harshly, as if it's in pain or just hungry. Either way, the cat grabs Leon's attention.

> LEON (V.O.)
> ...there was a cat. It wouldn't stop crying.

Leon stops crying. Listens to the cat's cries. They share a glance. Both of their eyes, equal in light and color. Both glowing like iridescent pearls in the stark darkness.

> LEON (V.O.) (CONT'D)
> So, I made it stop.

A loud THUD against the concrete -- Leon stands and walks over to the soundless cat, now lying on its side, its body completely turned to stone.

Leon drops to his knees, cries.

> LEON (CONT'D)
> No! No! No!

> LEON (V.O.) (CONT'D)
> I tried to reverse what was done. It was...

INT. STORAGE ROOM, AERODYNE - DAY - PRESENT DAY

With a scowl on his face, Leon faces Marcus.

> LEON
> ...<u>irreversible</u>.

EXT. ALLEYWAY, DOWNTOWN KANDY - NIGHT - FLASHBACK

Leon picks up the cat. Shakes it. It doesn't move an inch.

> LEON
> (screaming)
> Fuck!

Leon throws the cat against the wall, shattering it to pieces.

INT. STORAGE ROOM, AERODYNE - DAY - PRESENT DAY

After a moment of silence, Leon hangs his head.

> MARCUS
> Do the tests, Leon. And just maybe things will
> go back to the way they were before.

EXT. LANDING STRIP - DAY

Marcus steps out of the back of a black town car, rubbing his red eyes. Still
groggy from the drugs. He nods to the chauffeur.

The car speeds off, as Marcus walks to the private jet.

Along the way, he checks the GPS map on his phone. Zooms in on the map.
Finds the red ICON from the tracking device located in the middle of the desert.

INT. RECREATIONAL ROOM, AERODYNE - DAY

Ten years later.

Gathered around the hospital bed is a team of DOCTORS, including Bee. On the bed lies test subject, ALAN BIRCH.

Bee moves the pen from Alan's heel to his toes, which causes Alan to wiggle his toes underneath the bed sheet.

> ALAN
> (out of breath)
> It's cold...

> BEE
> How about this?

The doctor peels back the sheet and presses the pen against his calf; and then Alan feverishly bobs his head.

> ALAN
> Yes. I can feel it. I can feel it...

Alan motions to the nurse, a young black man named JAMES.

> ALAN (CONT'D)
> Please, James, I want to feel the floor beneath my feet.

James removes the bed sheet, helps Alan from the bed.

> BEE
> James, it's too soon --

> ALAN
> It's okay, Doc. James will catch me if I fall. Won't you, James?

Alan smiles. James smiles back.

> JAMES
> I got you, A Man.

James helps Alan to his feet. Walks to the open window where an artificial sun hangs over a distant mountaintop. James guides Alan, ready to catch Alan if he falls.

As Alan arrives at the sunrise before him, a roar of claps and cheers fill the room.

James stands back. Beams from ear to ear.

> ALAN (O.S.)
> (ecstatically)
> I can't believe it! I'm walking! I'm walking!

INT. OBSERVATIONAL ROOM E, AERODYNE - CONTINUOUS

With his arms crossed, Leon stands alone behind the mirror and watches the subject, Alan, admiring the sunset. Sighs. Then storms away; however, we don't see Leon's face.

INT. FOYER, THE BIRCH HOUSEHOLD - DAY

The front door opens.

On the front porch stands a healthy Alan, as well as TWO AGENTS, both dressed in suits, heavily armed underneath, carrying Alan's luggage.

Alan's wife, LAURA, opens the door. Cries. Then Alan's son, RYAN, eight years old, rushes from the KITCHEN.

> RYAN
> Dad!

Ryan hugs his father. Then Laura, now crying as well.

MONTAGE - ALAN READJUSTING TO DAILY LIFE

-- EXT. BACKYARD - DAY -- Alan and his son, Ryan, play catch while Laura watches from the kitchen window.

-- INT. KITCHEN - DAY -- Laura places the cup of coffee on the table and picks up the AERODYNE brochure, the front reading, "RESTORING A NATION, ONLY TO REBUILD A BRIGHTER FUTURE."

-- EXT. PORCH - DAY -- Alan returns from a jog around the neighborhood, his shirt doused in sweat, kisses Laura, who stands in a state of shock.

-- EXT. VORTEX VALLEY - DAY -- Laura crosses her arms and suspiciously watches Alan and Ryan, both throwing popcorn at one another as they move through a crowded amusement park.

-- INT. DINING ROOM - NIGHT -- Alan excuses himself from the table as Laura stands from the seat. Then Alan returns from the kitchen with a bottle of red wine. She smiles. Then he smiles.

INT. MASTER BEDROOM, THE BIRCH HOUSEHOLD - NIGHT

Two empty glasses of red wine remain on the dresser. We pan from the dresser to the floor and find articles of clothing, starting from shirts to pants to underwear to bras, all scattered madly throughout the room.

On the bed Alan is really giving it to Laura. So much that Laura has to shield her face with a pillow to keep herself from waking up Ryan in the next room. Their naked bodies, both drenched with sweat.

> LAURA
> (whispering)
> Right there, right there. Oh my God, Alan...

Alan relentlessly pounds away at Laura, never switching from the missionary position. Finally climaxes while on top of Laura.

Time passes. Hours. Both Alan and Laura flop against the bed. Labored breath. Laura can't remove the smile from her face. Alan, as dry as a bone.

> LAURA (CONT'D)
> (out of breath)
> What in the world did they do to you, Alan?

Laura slaps Alan on the arm.

> LAURA (CONT'D)
> We haven't gone that long since college.

Alan laughs, bobs his head.

                         ALAN
                     (excitedly)
        It's amazing, Laura. I feel like my old self again.

Alan leans over. Kisses Laura.

                     ALAN (CONT'D)
        I love you.

                         LAURA
        I love you too.

Laura pauses. Thinks for a moment.

                     LAURA (CONT'D)
                    (biting her lip)
             Wanna go again...

Alan can't resist. Sips from a glass of water on the nightstand. Then, they go
again.

INT. LABORATORY, AERODYNE - NIGHT

The scientist, DOCTOR KOVORSKY, finds a dead mouse in a cage. The
mouse is lying in a puddle of its own blood. Its body, completely contorted.

INT. OFFICE, LABORATORY - NIGHT

With a vacant expression on his face, David stands over the dead mouse on the
desk.

                         DAVID
                     (bitterly)
        How much time do we have?

                 DOCTOR KOVORSKY (O.S.)
        Not long, sir.

                         DAVID
        What's going to happen to Mr. Birch?

                 DOCTOR KOVORSKY
        I'm afraid it's only a matter of time before his
        body rejects the serum and then...

                        DAVID
            Then what?

The doctor draws his eyes toward the dead mouse.

INT. BEDROOM, THE BIRCH HOUSEHOLD - NIGHT

While Laura is passed out, Alan wakes with a sudden gasp!

Sweating profusely, Alan bolts upright.

                        ALAN
                    (murmuring)
            Oh God...

Alan rolls out of bed.

INT. BATHROOM, THE BIRCH HOUSEHOLD - CONTINUOUS

Alan flips on the light. Peers into the mirror. First, it starts with a nosebleed. Then, the shakes. His hand starts shaking, slowly at first and then violently. Alan studies his hand with great panic. Then, his fingers snap backward and shift out of place, causing Alan to scream in horror.

As the rest of his fingers shift out of place -- each joint as well -- Alan draws his wide eyes toward the mirror, only to witness his jaw being dislocated.

                    LAURA (O.S.)
            Alan? Is everything all right?

Alan falls to the floor, bleeding from every orifice in his body, now left crippled and contorted.

Laura rushes into the bathroom. Sees her husband dead on the floor. Screams bloody horror...

EXT. THE BIRCH HOUSEHOLD - NIGHT

Police cruisers surround the front of the house, the sirens blanketing it with a light show of reds and blues.

Standing among the OFFICERS are Laura and Ryan. Crying.

One OFFICER escorts Laura and Ryan to the cruiser in the driveway. Both Laura and Ryan are clinging to one another.

Watching from the front porch is seasoned detective CHUCK RIGSBY, 50's, white fellow, seasoned, slumped shoulders, trench coat. Next to him stands a younger detective, WAYNE PERSEY, 30's, black, bearded, level-headed.

> PERSEY
> You think she did it?

Rigsby turns toward his partner. Sighs.

> RIGSBY
> In all my years in the force, I've never seen
> anything like that before...
> (closely)
> ...Whoever it is, it's not human.

Rigsby walks away. Head down. Persey doesn't follow. Instead, he turns toward the open doorway behind him. Too afraid to enter.

INT. CONFERENCE ROOM, AERODYNE - NIGHT

David's assistant, TODD BISHOP, late 20's, tosses a pile of PHOTOGRAPHS on the table.

IN THE PHOTO

Alan's body is badly contorted underneath a pool of blood.

BACK TO TODD

who stands behind David.

> TODD
> What are we going to do with the wife and kid?

David stands in front of the window, which displays a glimmering skyline of New York City.

> TODD (CONT'D)
> Sir?

He turns his shoulder, switches off the projection with a handheld remote control. The windows fade to black, then light up with a bleak whiteness.

> DAVID
> Leave no traces. Understood?

> TODD
> (clearing his throat)
> Yes, sir.

Todd bows, then exits.

David walks across the vast room. Stands over the table. Picks up one photograph, which appears different from the other crime scene photos; in fact, one taken from a distance.

IN THE PHOTO

Laura and Ryan are standing in the front lawn. Hugging one another. Red and blue lights all around them.

BACK TO DAVID

who takes another sip of scotch.

INT. BREAK ROOM, PRECINCT 13 - NIGHT

With nobody looking, Persey squeezes two drops from a DROPPER, one into the cup of coffee and another into a carton of chocolate milk. Closes the lid of the milk. Shakes it. Then, lastly, he stirs the poison into the coffee.

INT. INTERROGATION ROOM, PRECINCT 13- NIGHT

Persey enters the room while Rigsby sits with Laura at the table. Places the lethal cup of coffee in front of Laura.

> PERSEY
> (vacantly)
> Here you go, ma'am. Cream. No sugar.

                        LAURA
            Thank you.

Laura picks up the coffee with both hands. Sips diligently.

INT. TESTING ROOM B, AERODYNE - DAY

We see the backside of Leon seated in a chair. Again, Leon's hooked up to all
kinds of machines. He's wearing a contraption over his head -- similar to
speculums, only much bulkier.

As we close in on a weakened Leon, we finally see his pale face, as blank as a
canvas. His eyes, bloodshot. The iris, now powder blue, has neither a circular
pattern nor its trademark glow. Yet, the iris remains unbound, the outer part
crumbling away from the pupil and chewing through all of the white in his eyes.

Along the side of Leon's neck, we see what looks like a growth of an infection --
the skin around the infection is scaly too.

At the other side of the room sits a sickly elephant.

                        LEON
                    (mumbling)
            I can't.

Bee walks over to Leon, gently touches him on the hand, which remains inside a
metal clasp on the armrest. So too does the other hand, restrained.

                        BEE
                    (tenderly)
            For me, Leon. Please.

Leon draws his unblinking eyes toward Bee's hand, then her pleasing eyes. Cracks
open his mouth.

Bee places a scale torn from Medusa's cheek on the tip of Leon's tongue. He
downs it with a sip of water from Bee's ASSISTANT. Both step away. Bee nods
to the mirror. Walks behind the safety barrier next to Leon.

INT. OBSERVATIONAL ROOM B, AERODYNE - CONTINUOUS

One of the lawyers, EDWIN, turns to David, who stands with his arms crossed.

                    EDWIN
          Why use a replica?

                    DAVID
          Why does a magician use objects to perform a
          trick?

Edwin shrugs.

                    EDWIN
          Distraction.

With a grin on his face, David faces Edwin.

                    DAVID
          Illusions, Edwin. We demonstrate to Leon that
          the gaze can only be released to its fullest potential
          by ingesting the scale. Take the classic hat trick.
          Now, let's apply that to Leon. The rabbit is his
          gaze. And the scale, well, that's his top hat.

                    EDWIN
          I'm confused.

David pats Edwin on the back.

                    DAVID
               (nodding to Leon)
          Just watch.

INT. TESTING ROOM B, AERODYNE - CONTINUOUS

The ENGINEER presses a red button outside a secured barrier.

A sudden CURRENT of electricity runs through Leon's body, causing every
muscle to tighten. The veins in his neck and forehead swell. Face, now red and
grimacing. Both eyes whiten, in their entirety.

As Leon gazes the elephant, the needle attached to the vein in his forearm
automatically feeds blood into the bag next to him; however, the blood is as dark
and thick as tar.

INT. LABORATORY, AERODYNE - DAY

The head scientist, DOCTOR SERVAL, late 50's, receding hairline, glasses, carefully places the vial of blood into a mixer. Turns on the machine.

INT. TESTING ROOM A, AERODYNE - CONTINUOUS

In a dimly lit room, more tests are conducted on Leon -- this one intended to provoke a seizure from Leon, as bright lights and strange perverted images flash in front of his eyes.

INT. LABORATORY, AERODYNE - CONTINUOUS

Doctor Serval removes the vial from the machine. Places a drop of blood on a slide and places the slide underneath a microscope.

UNDER THE MICROSCOPE

Leon's blood attacks the subject's cells, turns them into stone, and then, after a couple of tense seconds, regenerates the cells to normal.

BACK TO DOCTOR SERVAL

who removes his eye from the lens.

>   DOCTOR SERVAL (V.O.)
>   Think of the nervous system as an electrical grid,
>   or a network, and the nerves as transformers,
>   which distribute the energy.

INT. CORRIDOR, AERODYNE - DAY

Doctor Serval tries to keep pace with David. They pass a forklift carrying a statue of an elephant into a storage bay.

>   DOCTOR SERVAL
>   Leon's blood restores energy to the nerves;
>   however, over time, the nerves, like transformers,
>   they overheat.

> DAVID
> (angrily)
> Enough with the fucking analogies. Are the
> subjects good to go? Yes or no?

> DOCTOR SERVAL
> (hesitantly)
> No. I need more time, sir.

David stops, turns around, gets extremely close to Doctor Serval.

> DAVID
> Get it done or I'll find someone who will.

MONTAGE - THE TESTING SPEEDS UP

-- INT. HOSPITAL ROOM - DAY -- Doctor Serval injects Leon's blood into a sixty something year old patient, MARSHA HOWARD, paralyzed from the waist down.

-- INT. TESTING ROOM B - DAY -- Leon is zapped over and over until his gaze is released, then his blood drips into a vial.

-- EXT. PARK - DAY -- Marsha pushes her GRANDSON in a swing on a playground.

-- INT. TESTING ROOM A - DAY -- Images of war flash over Leon's eyes.

-- INT. KITCHEN - NIGHT -- Detective Rigsby stands over Marsha's contorted dead body, kneels down, and shakes his head in utter disgust.

-- INT. HOSPITAL ROOM - DAY -- The next patient, DALE GIBSON, 20's, Army veteran, walks for the first time in three years after returning home from overseas.

-- EXT. STREET - DAY -- Crowds cheer on Dale Gibson as he crosses the finish line of the CITY MARATHON.

-- INT. CONFERENCE ROOM - NIGHT -- David stands in front of a window, stares out at the gaudy skyscrapers of Tokyo, Japan.

-- INT. DALE'S APARTMENT - DAY -- Detective Rigsby pulls his eyes from the Army photograph on the wall and draws his attention toward a flyer for AERODYNE on the kitchen counter.

-- INT. HOSPITAL ROOM - DAY -- David sits by his father's bedside. Joseph Zappin is hooked up to a breathing machine. Unconscious.

-- INT. LEON'S SUITE - NIGHT -- Leon opens the door where he finds Bee standing in the hallway; she turns; and in her arms, she carries a casserole. She greets Leon with a smile.

-- INT. RIGSBY CAR - NIGHT -- As the detective studies the crime scene photos, a silhouette appears in the backseat; and as Rigsby turns his eyes toward the rear view mirror, a wire suddenly wraps around his neck, strangling him to death.

-- INT. OFFICE - NIGHT -- An exhausted Doctor Serval sips from coffee, pushes aside his patient's records, and then comes across one of Doctor Monaghan's patients, Sam. He reads the record, then he sits upright, eyes light up...

-- INT. LABORATORY - DAY -- Doctor Serval examines the slide of blood through the microscope. Removes his eyes. Drops his jaw in awe.

INT. HALLWAY, AERODYNE - NIGHT

Both Doctor Serval and David stand behind a pane of glass, observing the young child, SAM, sitting on the edge of the hospital bed.

> DOCTOR SERVAL (O.S.)
> Sixty-eight days and counting, sir.

Confused, David turns to the doctor.

> DAVID
> Why him? What makes him so special?

> DOCTOR SERVAL
> Similar to an antivenom, his body creates an
> immune response, creates antibodies to fight
> against Leon's blood. Then, the Medusa strain
> stays dormant inside the child, unlike the adult
> subjects.

> DAVID
> How sure are you?

DOCTOR SERVAL
One hundred percent.

DAVID
Move to phase three.

INT. 7TH STREET BAR - DAY

The place is empty, except for a couple of local PATRONS lethargically sipping from their drinks. The BARTENDER stops wiping down the bar and turns his head toward the BREAKING NEWS report on the television. Each head at the bar cranes upward as well. Eyes, now glued to the screen above.

ON THE TV

Stands a reporter, NANCY KELLOGG, in front a hospital.

REPORTER (ON TV)
This morning, Joseph Zappin, the CEO of Zappin Petroleum, passed away due to complications after being hospitalized at Saint Gabriel where he was being treated for pneumonia.

BACK TO THE BAR

The bartender tosses a rag over his shoulder.

BARTENDER
You guys wanna watch this or Slaughterhouse Five?

The bartender grabs the remote. Waits for a response.

PATRON (O.S.)
(slurring)
Slaughterhouse.

INT. LIVING ROOM, MARCUS'S APARTMENT - DAY

The blinds are closed; however, the only light on Marcus's face is the glow from the television.

> REPORTER (ON TV)
> During those twelve years, Mr. Zappin was a
> contributor to over a dozen charities around the
> world, including eCross and Light Way, which
> supplied over a million homes in Africa with clean
> and renewable energy. Mr. Zappin was also
> widely known for the controversial --

Teary-eyed, Marcus switches OFF the television. Throws the remote against the wall, shattering it to pieces.

INT. BATHROOM, LEON'S SUITE - NIGHT

On the toilet sits a naked Bee. She pushes, then winces. Pulls out a small plastic container from underneath her groin. Holds the container to her face.

As Bee anxiously nibbles on the corner of her lip -- one leg rapidly bouncing against floor -- she examines Leon's sperm inside the container.

> BEE
> (finally)
> Screw it.

Bee grabs the green cap from the sink and places it over the container. Seals it tightly.

INT. BEDROOM, LEON'S SUITE - CONTINUOUS

Leon stands at the moonlit window. Naked. Peers at the artificial moon suspended over the eastern coast of Maine. The bathroom door opens behind him. Leon turns his shoulder, finds Bee standing at the doorway, her body as dark as a silhouette behind the amber light.

> LEON
> Is everything all right?

                    BEE
Yeah. Fine. Just got a little light-headed. That's
all.

Bee pauses, clears her throat.

                  BEE (CONT'D)
I should go. If they found out I was here --

                  LEON
Do you want to go?

Finally, he turns away from the holographic moon; then strolls over to the bed.
Bee lies down as well. Slithers into Leon's arms. He slides his hand over her
cheek. Kisses the other cheek. Bee places her hand over Leon's hand.

Once more, Leon kisses Bee, this time on the lips.

                  BEE
Leon, you don't understand what this company is
capable of doing. Whatever this thing is between
us -- is it really worth compromising everything
we've accomplished in these past ten years?

Leon pulls himself from Bee, sits against the headboard.

Bee notices Leon's neck in the pale moonlight. The infection is no longer red;
however, the skin is scalier than before. She moves her hand down to Leon's
chest, her fingers now playing with his chest hair.

                  BEE (CONT'D)
What does it feel like, you know, when it
happens?

                  LEON
Imagine the pain you get when you burn the tip
of your finger with a match. Then imagine that
pain covering your entire body like a blanket...
            (eyes watering)
...Then the pressure sets in, starting from your
head, echoing down into your lungs, suffocating
your every breath...

Leon turns to Bee, witnesses the soft glow cast from the moonlight trapped in her
eyes. He cracks open his mouth, tempted to speak from his heart.

> BEE
> I'm so sorry, Leon. I didn't know.

A tense silence swells over the conversation. Leon turns away from Bee and stares at the painting, THE SON OF MAN by Rene Magritte, on the wall.

We close in on the apple in front of the MAN'S FACE; however, the apple is darker than its original green color.

INT. DAVID'S OFFICE, AERODYNE - CONTINUOUS

Guarding the entranceway perch two large statues of pharaohs, one of Sekhmet and the other of Ptah, holding a scepter.

We move forward into the massive office, closing in on David, who stands with his arms crossed in front of a panel of monitors.

The glow of the monitor highlights the shadows of his stern face. From the surveillance camera, he keenly watches Leon and Bee lying in the bed.

INT. CORRIDOR, AERODYNE - DAY

The door to TESTING ROOM C automatically opens, then TWO GUARDS exit with Leon dangling from their arms. Leon is covered in sweat, panting, trembling...

Bee excuses herself from another DOCTOR and rushes to Leon.

> BEE
> I can take it from here, guys.

As the guards let go of a weakened Leon, Bee wraps her arm around him, sits him down, and then places a cool towel over his neck.

> BEE (CONT'D)
> The supplements are making your condition
> worse. I have to confront David about this or else
> --

LEON
(with his head down)
-- Like you give a shit about what happens to me.
You're just like the rest of them.

BEE
I'm not --

Bee turns to the other DOCTORS. Witnesses two of them whispering in secret, as well as shooting glances at her.

BEE (CONT'D)
(quietly now)
-- I'm not like them, Leon. When are you ever
going to see that? I <u>do</u> care.

Bee leans closer. Gets a better look at Leon's eyes, which remain tightly shut. She pulls out a flashlight from her coat pocket. Partially opens one eyelid. Shines the light in Leon's eye. The right pupil is completely ripped in half.

With his scaly hand, he grabs her hand before he can look her directly in the eyes. She carefully lowers the flashlight.

INT. RECOVERY ROOM, AERODYNE - DAY

Sipping from a glass of water, Leon sits on the edge of the table. A door opens from behind. David enters. The NURSE -- struggling to make eye contact with David -- exits.

DAVID (O.S.)
Hello, Leon...

David paces around Leon, who is much calmer now. The shaking is gone. The sweating, gone. His eyes, much better as well.

DAVID (CONT'D)
...Bee told me what happened earlier today. I felt
so awful about what happened that I was
compelled to pay you a visit.

David places his hand over Leon's shoulder.

DAVID (CONT'D)
You gave us quite a scare, Leon.

                         LEON
        I lost control...

Leon turns his eyes toward David. A ghost of a glare on Leon's pale face.

                    LEON (CONT'D)
        ...It won't happen again.

                      DAVID
        Let's hope not. I have a lot invested in you,
        Leon...
                (patting Leon's shoulder)
        ...I'll let you rest.

David walks away.

                      LEON
             (over his shoulder)
        Sorry to hear about your father.

A smirk on David's face. He stops for a moment, as he looks over his shoulder and steals a glance from Leon. Then, he walks away. Again.

INT. CONTAINMENT ROOM, AERODYNE - DAY

Leon stands in front of the pane of glass. Stares at Medusa's head. He turns to the once heavily secured door at the end of the hallway. No guards around.

INT. DAVID'S OFFICE, AERODYNE - CONTINUOUS

From the surveillance camera, David carefully watches Leon walking down the hallway.

                      DAVID
             (to himself)
        Good boy.

INT. HOLDING CELLS, AERODYNE - CONTINUOUS

Behind the door, Leon discovers a massive corridor with bare cells on each side. Similar to the testing rooms, the corridor is built with dense concrete walls.

As Leon strolls through the desolation, he comes across the first cell guarded by steel bars. Peeks inside.

Blood stains, Leon sees, dull and yet splattered against the walls of the cell. Noticeable, but just barely. Other stains as well. Not blood. As he kneels down, he finds a couple of old teeth on the floor of the ruined cell.

Then Leon proceeds forward. Comes across more cells. More bloodstains. More fragments left behind by the human body.

Suddenly, from a distance, he hears the shrill scream of a WOMAN. Leon turns to the direction of the scream.

> LEON
> (mortified)
> Briana...

Following the screaming a SLAM of a metal door!

Leon rushes toward the scream; however, quietly and cautiously. He rounds a corner, only to find a closed door at the end of another HALLWAY.

More screaming, we hear, then a couple of soft THUDS coming from behind the closed door.

INT. TORTURE CHAMBER, AERODYNE - CONTINUOUS

The TORTURER throws another right hook across a WOMAN'S face. The woman, Leon sees behind the door window, is Bee. Her face is bruised and covered in blood.

Another MAN stands next to the torturer, slowly unbuckling his belt.

The torturer attempts to land yet another blow. He suddenly freezes during his strike downward. His fist inches from Bee's cheek. In the corner of his eye, he spots a FIGURE looming behind the door...

We see Leon behind the glass window. His eyes, all white, peering directly at the torturer, now screaming in terror as his right arm slowly turns to stone, starting from his knuckles to his shoulder blade.

The other man, an agent named CARL, keeps his eyes away from Leon and frantically reaches for a HELMET with a silver visor on the table. Fumbles the helmet. Then puts on the helmet. Backs himself up against the wall.

Then Leon enters the chamber, slowly. Grabs the torturer's right arm and kicks his body away. The torturer falls to the floor, bleeding and screaming. Leon holds the severed arm like a club.

> CARL
> Please! We were only following orders!

Leon rams the stoned fist into Carl's gut, forcing his body forward. Swings the arm down at Carl's head. The helmet drops from his head. He grabs Carl by his throat. Slams him against the wall. Uses his gaze. Carl's head turns to stone, only his head. The rest of his body falls limp.

Top heavy now, Carl crashes to the floor. Head first...

The head shatters on impact!

Leon hears Bee groaning from behind. Hurries to Bee, now clinging onto consciousness. Her face is hardly recognizable from all the blood.

Gently, Leon brushes her hair away from her closed eyes. Cups her fragile face in his trembling hands. Takes a deep breath.

> LEON
> We have to get out of here...

Leon releases the shackles from her wrists, both tied around the backside of the chair. Holds her close.

The armless torturer laughs, as he slides along the floor. Finally, he props his body upright against the wall.

> TORTURER
> (resonantly)
> Wherever you go, we'll find you. We own you,
> Leon. You're property of Aerodyne...

Leon turns to the torturer, now as pale as a ghost. A puddle of blood forming beneath his body. He stands Bee upright; she staggers, but Leon is there to keep her upright.

> LEON
> Let's get out of here...

INT. ZONE B, AERODYNE - DAY

Leon spots a couple of GUARDS at the end of the hallway. He readjusts his arm around Bee; then they both discreetly walk the other direction.

As they make it down another HALLWAY, an alarm blares out from above followed with sirens flashing yellow overhead.

> LEON
> What's that?

> BEE
> There's no way out, Leon --

Suddenly, a door automatically opens from the end of the hallway. Leon turns to the door.

> LEON
> I think we have somebody looking after us.
> Come on. This way...

They make their way through the door.

INT. EMERGENCY ELEVATORS - DAY

Both Leon and Bee ride the elevator to the surface.

> LEON
> Is something wrong?

Bee turns to Leon with a worried expression on her face.

> BEE
> They're making it too easy for us.

> LEON
> I know. That's what scares me.

INT./EXT. FLORAL SHOP - DAY

The elevator doors open, then Leon and Bee step from the elevators. Both cautious. They look around at a vast spread of various flowers scattered around the store.

> LEON
> Looks like we're back in Eden.

> BEE
> I can't even remember the last time I've seen the surface. I almost forgot what it felt like to breathe real air.

Leon blows the dust from the top of a rose.

> LEON
> Yeah. Me too.

They check the front door. Locked. Bee turns to the cash register. Checks the computer screen.

Meanwhile, Leon tries to find something heavy to throw through the front window.

> BEE (O.S.)
> Leon...

Leon walks to Bee, who is pointing at the screen, which is flashing "SECURITY BREACH."

We see a SUV cruising down MAIN STREET. Then, in the corner of Leon's eye, he catches the SUV.

> LEON
> (abruptly)
> Get down!

Leon and Bee take cover behind the front counter as the SUV drives past the store. He pokes his head from the counter. Finds a table cloth on a table. Wraps the cloth around his fist and then, as quietly as he can, breaks the front window.

LEON (CONT'D)

Come on.

He clears away the glass, then guides Bee through the door.

LEON (CONT'D)

We need to find a car.

Bee nods.

BEE

I know a garage not far from here --

As they proceed down the sidewalk, a sudden explosion erupts from behind a building.

INT. ALLEYWAY, EDEN - CONTINUOUS

Leon and Bee take cover, as a ball of flames curls into the sky. Following the explosion, an audience of gunfire clapping not too far away.

Leon and Bee rush down the alleyway -- away from the gunfire.

Halfway down the alley, the same SUV suddenly skids in front of them, preventing them from passing. The passenger door opens, the strange driver steps out. Both Leon and Bee spin around and run the opposite way. Then...

A gunshot rings out, forcing Leon and Bee dead in their tracks!

They both rotate around, Leon checking for any injuries but finding none. There, at the other end of the alley, they see the chauffeur falling to his knees, an eddy of smoke emitting from the bullet hole in his forehead.

The chauffeur falls to the ground, revealing Marcus with a smoking revolver aimed ahead. He lowers the revolver to his waist-side. Nods at Leon.

LEON

Marcus?

MARCUS

Are you two just going to stand there or do you want to get the hell out of here?

84

                    BEE
          Is he with you?

Leon nods; then they walk over to Marcus. Leon stops and stands over the dead chauffeur. Notices a couple of sparks spitting from the bullet hole.

                    BEE (O.S.) (CONT'D)
          What is it?

                    LEON
               (to Bee)
          Nothing. Let's go.

INT. SUV - DAY

Marcus drives while Leon and Bee ride in the backseat. They make a turn off Main Street and meet up with two other men, LUCAS and HARPER, standing outside a flaming vehicle.

                    MARCUS
          Don't worry. They're with me.

Marcus parks next to the vehicle, then turns to Leon.

                    MARCUS (CONT'D)
               (exiting SUV)
          Wait here.

                    BEE
               (to Leon)
          How do you know this guy?

                    LEON
          I don't exactly <u>know</u> him. His name's Marcus
          Hopkins. He found me while I was living in
          Kandy. He was the one who brought me here. I
          remember he said he was a recruiter for Aerodyne.

                    BEE
          Whoever he is, he doesn't work for Aerodyne.

EXT. STREET - CONTINUOUS

Marcus stands over the two GUARDS, both dead.

                    LUCAS
          What's next, sir?

                    MARCUS
                (to Lucas)
          We hide.

INT. SUV - NIGHT

As they ride down a dirt road surrounded by woods, Leon and Bee remain in silence. Bee slides closer to Leon. He holds her in his arms. Marcus moves his eyes toward the rear view mirror.

EXT. CROW'S NEST RANCH - NIGHT

The sun falls behind the caps of mountains. They ride down a long gravel road until they reach an open field surrounded by a lush forest, consisting of mostly pine trees; and behind the forest, rolling hills, which makes for a pleasant view. Two houses, a cabin and a smaller house behind the cabin. A small barn as well, tucked behind the cabin.

As Marcus parks in front of the cabin, the motion sensors kick on, casting a light on the front PORCH of the house.

INT. SUV - CONTINUOUS

Marcus switches off the ignition.

                    LEON
          Where are we?

                    MARCUS
          Home...
                (to Leon)
          ...For now, at least.

EXT. CROW'S NEST RANCH - CONTINUOUS

All three walk up the front steps of the porch, Leon staying extra cautious. Bee slips her hand into Leon's hand and stays close to him.

INT. FOYER, CABIN - CONTINUOUS

Marcus switches on each lamp and turns on every light. The place is very homey. Walls made from oak. A large bookshelf stocked with a year's worth of reading material. A fireplace made of stone is probably the nicest feature of the house.

>   MARCUS
>   Make yourself at home.

>   LEON
>   Where's the bathroom?

>   MARCUS
>   Just down the hall. On the right.

INT. BATHROOM, CABIN - NIGHT

Leon grabs the first aid kit from the medicine cabinet as Bee sits down on the toilet seat. He turns on the faucet and runs the gauze underneath the water. Clears away the dry blood caked above Bee's eyebrows.

>   BEE
>   (grabbing Leon's hand)
>   Leon, I don't trust him.

Leon lowers his hand. Drains the blood into the sink.

>   LEON
>   Yeah. I don't either. But what other choice do
>   we have?

As Leon wipes away the blood from Bee's chin, she grabs his hand yet again. He pulls his hand away, carefully.

>   BEE
>   Back at Aerodyne, why did you keep pursuing
>   me?

Leon gives the question a moment to marinate; then he looks into Bee's eyes.

> LEON
> I think you know why?

> BEE
> No. I don't. I want you to tell me. Please,
> Leon...

Bee reaches toward Leon's hand; however, Leon pulls away. Stands to his feet. His back, now facing Bee.

> BEE (CONT'D)
> You can't even say the words. Can you?

Leon places the gauzes on the sink and leaves.

INT. LIVING ROOM, CABIN - NIGHT

A couple of NOISES coming from the kitchen: the sound of glass cups being placed over wood and then the sound of a cabinet closing.

Leon wanders around, mostly scoping out the place, as Marcus makes the coffee. Leon finds a picture frame on the fireplace mantle.

IN THE PICTURE

Joseph Zappin stands next to Marcus, both of them decked out in hunting gear. Rifles resting over their shoulders. Both smiling. Both appear extremely close.

BACK TO LEON

who turns to the kitchen.

Marcus exits the kitchen with two cups of coffee in his hand. Then Bee, now bandaged up, exits the bathroom.

Leon paces around. Turns to Marcus.

> LEON
> No TV?

> MARCUS
> No TV. No landline. No computer. No cell
> phones. We're officially off the grid.

First, Marcus hands Bee the cup of the coffee and then Leon. At first, Leon is leery about drinking the coffee.

>   MARCUS (CONT'D)
>   That's the whole point. Right?

Leon doesn't respond.

>   MARCUS (CONT'D)
>   If there's an emergency, you can contact one of
>   my men. I'll have two guys working around the
>   clock.

>   LEON
>   I think we can manage.

>   MARCUS
>   I wasn't asking, Leon. Besides, it's for your own
>   good.

Leon sighs. Turns to Bee.

>   MARCUS (CONT'D)
>   You know, I used to frequent this cabin whenever
>   things got a little hectic. It belongs, well, did
>   belong to Joseph Zappin. Senior, that is. Only a
>   couple of people know about this place.

>   BEE
>   And would one of those people be his son?

>   MARCUS
>   I wouldn't have brought you two here if David
>   Zappin knew about it. Now, would I?
>   (nodding at the picture)
>   Joe used to bring me up here every fall to hunt.

Marcus sighs, looks down at the picture.

>   MARCUS (CONT'D)
>   After the accident, he handed down the cabin to
>   me. I come here from time to time. To clear
>   my head.

Leon turns to Marcus, studies his face.

INT. KITCHEN, CABIN - NIGHT

While Bee stands against the counter -- sipping from the coffee -- Marcus slides a manila folder in front of Leon. He opens the folder. Flips photos of test subjects, ranging from older to younger -- even as young as children -- all suffering from paralysis, locked in cells like stray dogs.

IN THE PHOTO

Over a hundred dead bodies being dumped into a massive hole in the desert.

BACK TO LEON

who grimaces from the sight of the photograph.

> MARCUS
> These were obtained by one of my men who is currently working undercover at Aerodyne.

> LEON
> (holding up the photo)
> What the hell is this?

> MARCUS
> Unlike his father who dedicated nearly his entire life to research, David Zappin wasn't trying to find a cure. Instead, he was trying to design a weapon; and as far as we know, he is <u>that</u> close to making that weapon a reality.

> MARCUS (CONT'D)
> What kind of weapon?

Marcus shows Leon a photo of a strange glass box, one half of the contraption hooked up to wires, which feed into servers.

> MARCUS (CONT'D)
> That was taken a week ago.

> LEON
> What is it?

                    MARCUS
        We don't exactly know, yet. But whatever it is,
        you're the final piece.

Bee picks up one particular photo from the other photographs, places her hand
over her mouth in shock. Leon notices Bee's stunning reaction.

                    BEE
        David told me he was transferred to a
        rehabilitation facility outside Eugene.

                    MARCUS
        Well, then you weren't the only one who was
        deceived by David Zappin.

                    LEON
        Did you know these people?

                    BEE
        Just this one. His name was Sam. He was a
        patient of mine.

Bee paces around the kitchen, looking down at the photo of the dead boy -- and
he's <u>not</u> contorted like the others.

                    MARCUS
        After Joe found out his son was conducting these
        experiments, he had to stop him; and since
        Aerodyne is one of the most heavily guarded
        facilities in the country, we needed to find a way
        inside.

INT. BOB'S HARDWARE - DAY - FLASHBACK

Leon turns to Marcus, staggering in front of the door. Two guards separating the
two of them. Marcus rubs his eyes, still groggy from the drugs.

                    MARCUS (V.O.)
        You, Leon.

INT. KITCHEN, CABIN - DAY - PRESENT DAY

Marcus leans closer.

                    MARCUS
            You were my way in.

Marcus gives Leon a chance to respond. Doesn't. Yet, he tries to absorb
everything on his plate, in essence.

                MARCUS (CONT'D)
        I'm sorry, Leon. It was the only way we could
        find out what David Zappin was really up to.

Leon flips through the photos, comes across a crime scene photo of a dead Alan
Birch, his bloody, contorted body. Silence builds.

                MARCUS (CONT'D)
        Alan Birch. That happened three days after Mr.
        Birch was discharged from Aerodyne.

                    LEON
        I saw this man walk with my own eyes. He was
        cured.

Leon turns to Bee. Holds up the photo of Alan.

                LEON (CONT'D)
                (now angrily)
        Did you know about this?

Bee walks to Leon. Grabs photograph. Face goes empty.

                    BEE
            No.

Bee sits down next to Leon. Eyes still attached to the photograph.

EXT. PORCH, CABIN - NIGHT

Leon stands against the railing, staring at the stars above. Marcus approaches from
behind.

                    MARCUS
        I hate to be the bearer of bad news.

Marcus hands Leon a beer.

                    LEON
          I don't drink.

                    MARCUS
          Suit yourself.

Marcus sits down in the rocking chair, sips from his beer.

                    LEON
          So, this is it?

                    MARCUS
          For now, yes.

Marcus sips, then points at Leon.

                    MARCUS (CONT'D)
          Joe and I used to hang out right here. He'd stand
          where you're at and look up at the stars.

                    LEON
          Were you two close?

                    MARCUS
          Practically raised me as if I was his own. He was
          a good man, Joe was...
                    (clearing his throat)
          ...When he found me on the streets, I was
          nothing. Just another kid tossed aside like
          garbage. Left to survive in the gutters. Joe gave
          me an opportunity. And now I'm passing along
          the torch to you.

Leon thinks to himself while Marcus takes another sip of his drink. Squints his
eye.

                    MARCUS (CONT'D)
          You know, if I didn't know any better, you seem
          as if you miss that place.

A sigh from Leon; then he directs his glimmering eyes toward the crescent moon.

                    LEON
          Where did the time go?

> MARCUS
> You'd be surprised how much things change in a
> decade.

Leon looks around.

> LEON
> (somberly)
> It all looks the same to me.

INT. LIVING ROOM, CABIN - NIGHT

Bee lies underneath a wool quilt in front of the fireplace. A low fire burns before
her.

> LEON (O.S.)
> How are you holding up?

> BEE
> I found out that the last eighteen years of my life
> was a lie.

Leon slips underneath the quilt; lies next to Bee.

> BEE (CONT'D)
> All this time, I thought I was doing some good in
> the world. Little did I know I was just helping
> destroy it. How do you think I'm holding up?

He pulls Bee close to his body. Strokes her hair.

> LEON
> Not all of those years were a lie.

Bee rolls around, faces Leon. Tears build in Bee's eyes. They kiss and hold each
other in the glow of the warm fire.

EXT. PORCH, CABIN - DAY

Marcus puts on his shades. Looks at the mountains in the distance. Shakes
Leon's hand.

> MARCUS
>
> I'll check in as often as I can. You and Briana
> make a list of whatever you need -- food, toilet
> paper, supplies, whatever, and give it to one of
> the guys.

Marcus points at one of the two men standing guard at the end of the driveway.

> MARCUS (CONT'D)
>
> Think of it this way: it'll feel as if you're taking
> an extending vacation. After everything y'all have
> been through, I think it's the least y'all deserve.

Marcus walks to the SUV. Drives away.

INT. FOYER, CABIN - DAY

Bee closes the door behind her, faces Leon.

> LEON
>
> So, I was thinking maybe --

Leon leaps at Bee, kisses her on the cheek and then the neck. They both remove their shirts. Leon picks her up and carries her to the couch.

MONTAGE - BEE FALLING IN LOVE WITH LEON

-- INT. LIVING ROOM - NIGHT -- From the flickering flames of the fire, we see the back of Bee. Her naked body is straddled over Leon's, her hips thrusting over his.

-- INT. KITCHEN - NIGHT -- Leon and Bee, now only wearing wrinkled shirts and socks, sit across from one another on the floor and laugh and eat cereal together.

-- EXT. FIELD - DAY -- Leon, bearded now, chases a giggling Bee; then Leon tackles Bee; Bee takes the better end of the fall and lands on top of Leon, runs her hands through his beard and kisses him.

-- EXT. FOREST - DAY -- Leon and Bee walk hand-in-hand down a windy trail; Bee points out a bird from above.

-- EXT. FOREST - DAY -- Leon reaches the treeline, waves Bee close; before them sits a small town in a valley.

-- INT. USED BOOKS STORE - DAY -- Leon and Bee browse the aisles; and as they duck into the MYSTERY SECTION, Leon pushes Bee against a shelf of books and kisses her.

INT. USED BOOKS, HILLSBORO - DAY

Leon places the novel, "FRANKENSTEIN," by Mary Shelley on the counter.

                    CASHIER
            Will that be all, sir?

Bee grabs a MOON BAR from the display case and places it on the counter. She turns to Leon, bats her eyelashes.

                    BEE
            Girl's gotta sweet tooth.

Leon wraps his arms around her waist. Pecks her on the neck.

                    LEON
            (whispers in her ear)
            Aren't I sweet enough?

Bee kisses Leon on the lips.

                    BEE
            You're plenty sweet.

                    CASHIER
            That will be ten dollars even.

Bee reaches in her pocket and hands the CASHIER a twenty dollar bill while Leon scans the rest of the library. His eyes cross an Internet café where a couple of STUDENTS are sipping from cups of coffee, googling, or whatever students do on computers.

Leon's eyes lock onto a WEBCAM next to a computer. He focuses on the camera. Eyes hone like blades. He gazes the webcam. Or does he? His face starts to tremble, slowly at first and then violently.

> BEE
> (petrified)
> Leon? Oh God...

As the cashier hands Bee the change, she grabs Leon by the arm. Faces him. Strings of blood rush from Leon's nose. Foam froths from the corners of his mouth. His eyes flicker, then slowly wash over with white.

Bee quickly covers her eyes before Leon mistakenly gazes her. Then, a booming HUM cuts through the store! Then...

Blackness fills the entire store!

> CASHIER
> (in the darkness)
> What in the world is going on?

Bee finds a pair of sunglasses on a rack and steals them without the cashier paying attention.

EXT. MAIN STREET, HILLSBORO - DAY

Bee guides Leon from the unlit bookstore. He's wearing sunglasses over his eyes; and he's still dazed from the recent seizure. A couple of pedestrians surface from the local stores on the strip and look around in bafflement.

The entire town is left without power; and it is all from what Leon did to the webcam! But what exactly did he do?

As both Leon and Bee round the intersection, the lights finally come back on, one by one. Then, street lights. Then, smartphones...

INT. DIAGNOSTICS ROOM, AERODYNE - DAY

The computer screen flashes, "ALERT!" The ENGINEER places the veggie wrap aside and rolls his chair toward the computer.

ON THE MONITOR

From the SATELLITE'S POV, we see <u>every</u> phone in Hillsboro light up with a blue dot, as radiant as a star. The dots rapidly flicker and spread from Hillsboro to the next town and the town after that, causing a chain reaction.

Finally, the surge of energy loses power once it reaches a large city. The dots fade out inside the city's infrastructure, then darken...

> ENGINEER
> (in awe)
> It worked. I can't believe it.

INT. MASTER BEDROOM, CABIN - NIGHT

As Leon rests his head against the pillow, Bee pats the top of his forehead with a cool washcloth.

> LEON
> That's not the first time that's happened to me.
> Do you remember the first night we spent
> together?

> BEE
> How can I forget?

> LEON
> Earlier that day, they were running a couple of
> tests on me. One of them was --

> BEE
> -- A retinal test. I remember David mentioning
> something about trying out a new code.
> Whatever he was talking about, it went beyond
> my head...

> LEON
> My body felt like it was going to explode. I was
> cold, almost numb. It was like -- I don't know --
> like I was outside my body.

QUICK FLASHES - LEON'S MEMORY

-- Columns of ones and zeroes stream across a sea of darkness.

-- Leon's eyes rapidly flicker, then roll in the back of his head.

-- A merry glint of light runs along a town's grid like "PAC MAN" screaming across narrow corridors -- flickering videos from everyday traffic cameras, webcams, surveillance cameras speed across his range of vision at a blinding speed.

> LEON (CONT'D)
> I felt...

Leon turns to Bee.

> LEON (CONT'D)
> (vacantly)
> ...<u>nothing</u>. I felt nothing.

EXT. FOREST - DAY

Both decked out in hunting gear, Marcus and Leon walk side by side through the trails. Both carry rifles over their shoulders.

> MARCUS
> Lucas told me you and Bee have been frequently
> visiting Hillsboro.

> LEON
> Bee's been having cabin fever lately.

> MARCUS
> (casually)
> Listen, Leon. I didn't come here to bark orders
> or make you two feel as if you're trapped here
> forever. All I'm saying is that you need to be
> more careful --

> LEON
> -- It's been over a year now, Marcus. Don't you
> think he's stopped looking.

MARCUS
People like David Zappin <u>don't</u> stop looking.

They stop walking. Face each other.

MARCUS (CONT'D)
I contacted my inside guy. Said he thinks
something big is going down at Aerodyne.
There's been more activity. They're bringing in
more security. My advice, Leon: stay close to
home for a few days. Can you do that for me?

LEON
Yeah. Sure. I'll tell Bee.

MARCUS
(nodding at Leon's beard)
By the way, what does she think about that thing?

LEON
This?

MARCUS
Not your style, Leon.

LEON
She wants me to shave it off.

Marcus laughs, then Leon joins in.

MARCUS
She's a smart woman.

He pats Leon on the back.

MARCUS (CONT'D)
Make sure she stays that way, my friend.

The excitement settles; Leon turns to Marcus.

LEON
Lately, I've been thinking.

MARCUS
This place will do that.

> LEON
> I've been thinking a lot about Kandy. The day
> you were captured.

Marcus hangs his head.

> MARCUS
> (disappointedly)
> I thought they told you.

> LEON
> The man who captured you. Hawsawi. Who
> was he? Really.

> MARCUS
> Aerodyne hired Hawsawi three years prior to your
> recruitment.

> LEON
> He worked for Aerodyne?

Marcus nods his head yes.

> MARCUS
> Hawsawi, along with a handful of others,
> including one of my men, was assigned to watch
> your every move. A couple of nights before I was
> captured, Hawsawi picked a fight with one of
> Aerodyne's senior officers. Killed him along with
> another employee who was trying to break up the
> fight. David wanted to find out if you were
> capable of working for Aerodyne by putting you
> in a 'Fight or Flight' situation.

> LEON
> So, he used me as an executioner?

> MARCUS
> Listen, Leon, I know you've been through the
> damn ringer. I can't tell you how many times I
> thought about telling you, but I was afraid it
> would jeopardize the mission.

Marcus faces Leon.

MARCUS (CONT'D)
I am sorry, Leon. <u>Truly</u>.

LEON
You were just doing your job --

MARCUS
Why did you come back for me, Leon?

Leon doesn't answer, at first.

MARCUS (CONT'D)
You could've used the passport I gave you and
gone anywhere you desired. But you stayed.
Why?

LEON
Maybe because I knew that one day we'd be
standing right here. Talking to each other as
friends, not enemies.

Marcus smiles and pats Leon on the shoulder.

INT. MASTER BEDROOM, CABIN - DAY

Bee rinses the toothpaste from her mouth, dries her face, and then exits the
bathroom. Leon lies on his side of the bed, reading the novel,
"FRANKENSTEIN."

BEE
(sitting next to Leon)
I'm going to have to come up with another
nickname for you other than Sasquatch.

She runs her hand over his recently shaved face and then kisses his cheek.

BEE (CONT'D)
You look so much better without it.

Leon closes the book. Bee bobs her head, smiles. They kiss.

> LEON

You think?

> BEE
> (while kissing Leon)

Oh yes. I was <u>thinking</u> about making a trip into town. We're getting low on milk.

> LEON
> (leaning back)

About that. Marcus said we need to keep our heads down for a few days.

Bee rolls out of bed, plants her hands over her hips as she shifts her weight to one side of her body.

> BEE

That man doesn't own us, Leon. We've been keeping our heads down for a year now. We should start --

> LEON

-- We wouldn't be alive if it wasn't for that man, Bee.

Bee storms to the dresser. Grabs her sweater.

> BEE

This is ridiculous. I'm not going to be a prisoner for the rest of my life.

Leon rolls out of bed. Stands aggressively.

> LEON

Is that what you think you are? A prisoner?

Bee sighs, removes her bra, and then puts on the sweater.

> BEE
> (while dressing)

I didn't mean it like that, Leon.

LEON
You have me, Bee. We have each other. Isn't
that enough?

BEE
It is, Leon. I just...

Bee scratches the top of her forehead. Sighs again.

BEE (CONT'D)
...I need some fresh air. Okay?

Bee exits.

LEON
Briana! Please...

INT. HALLWAY, CABIN - CONTINUOUS

Leon chases after Bee, now storming down the staircase. He leans over the
banister.

LEON
...I can't lose you.

Bee stands in the FOYER, looks up at Leon.

BEE
I'll be back later. Promise.

EXT. GUEST HOUSE - CONTINUOUS

Marcus steps from the front door. He stands on the porch and watches Bee get
inside a beat-up TRUCK in the barn.

INT. MASTER BEDROOM, CABIN - DAY

A couple of KNOCKS on the door! Leon turns away from the window and finds
Marcus standing at the doorway.

MARCUS
What's going on?

LEON
She just needs some space.

MARCUS
I'll have my men stop her --

LEON
(abruptly)
-- No. Let her go.

Marcus studies Leon's face, the anger brewing beneath.

MARCUS
I'll be downstairs, if you need me.

EXT. CONVENIENT STORE - NIGHT

We see a "CLOSED" sign on the front door. We pan from the sign and follow
HEADLIGHTS approaching from the south.

A black Rolls Royce -- tinted windows -- parks underneath a dim floodlight on the
corner of the gas station.

The back door opens; and out steps David from the backseat. He walks to a
shadowy figure waiting near a ice machine next to the store. The figure reveals
itself in the dim light...

DAVID
Didn't think you'd show.

Bee steps into the light. She pulls out a sealed bag from her pocket. Hands the
bag to David. He examines the drop of Leon's blood on a small, squared piece of
toilet paper.

DAVID (CONT'D)
This is it?

                    BEE
What did you do to him?

                    DAVID
     Do?

David slips the bag into the inner pocket of his sports coat.

                    DAVID (CONT'D)
We gave him a way out.

                    BEE
               (distressfully)
The other day, he asked me about an article I
wrote on molecular biology. I posted the article
four years ago on the Internet.

                    DAVID
He's now starting to see the 'bigger' picture...
               (stepping closer to Bee)
...In order to gain full <u>control</u> over Leon, first we
must understand what makes him twist and turn --

                    BEE
-- I did what you asked. Now, I want out. For
good.

                    DAVID
Of course. Consider this your resignation.

                    BEE
Then it's done. You'll leave us alone...

                    DAVID
You have feelings for him. Don't you?

Bee scowls from the remark.

                    BEE
Haven't you done enough with this man?

David steps even closer, removes his leather glove, and then runs the backside of
his hand across Bee's cheek.

DAVID
Oh, my dear, we've only scratched the surface...

He scratches Bee's chin with his fingernail. She flinches; her hand covers the tiny gash. She pulls away her finger. Glances at the blood on the tip of her finger.

A blank stare from David; then he applies his glove and walks back to the car.

INT. ROLLS ROYCE - CONTINUOUS

David shuts the door behind him. Seated next to David is a shadowy SMOKER, older -- late 50's perhaps -- an ashen color on his face. He takes a drag from the lit cigarette and blows the smoke from the cracked window.

SMOKER
Is she going to be a problem, Mr. Barros?

David tightens his jaw. Glares at the smoker.

DAVID
No.

SMOKER
And Leon?

DAVID
I'll use my imagination.

The smoker takes another drag. Exhales smoke.

INT. TRUCK - NIGHT

With the side of her hand, Bee wipes the tears from red eyes. She spots a pair of HEADLIGHTS in the rear view mirror. She sniffles the phlegm. Straightens her posture. Tightens her hands on the steering wheel. Moves her eyes back to the rear view mirror.

The car makes a right turn toward town; then Bee breathes a sigh of relief.

EXT. FOREST, CROW'S NEST - NIGHT

Lucas spots an oncoming truck.

> LUCAS
> (to his partner)
> Heads up.

He grabs the radio attached to his breast pocket.

INT. BEDROOM, GUEST HOUSE - CONTINUOUS

Marcus picks up the walkie-talkie, then walks to the window. Spots the truck at a distance.

INTERCUT - RADIO CONVERSATION

> LUCAS
> Sir, Ms. Monaghan has just arrived.

> MARCUS
> Was she followed?

> LUCAS
> Doesn't appear so.

> MARCUS
> Let her through...
> (another thought)
> ...And make sure you sweep the perimeter.

> LUCAS
> Yes, sir.

INT. MASTER BEDROOM, CABIN - NIGHT

As Leon lies on the bed, Bee slips into the bed, causing Leon to stir between the sheets. She wraps her arms around Leon's body. Holds him close.

                        LEON
             You feel better?

                        BEE
                    (calmly)
             Now, I do.

Bee sighs.

                        BEE (CONT'D)
             Leon?

                        LEON
             Yes.

                        BEE
             If I was to leave tomorrow, would you come with
             me?

Leon rolls to his other side. Faces Bee. Looks into her glossy eyes.

                        LEON
             Of course.

Leon places his hand over Bee's cheek.

                        LEON (CONT'D)
             I would follow you until the end of time.

                        BEE
             Two against the world.

                        LEON
                    (smiling)
             Two against the world.

Bee smiles too. A tear rolls down her cheek.

                        MARCUS (V.O.)
             Leon!

INT. BEDROOM, GUEST HOUSE - DAY

Sweating profusely, Marcus suddenly bolts upright from a dead sleep. Breath
extremely labored.

He pulls the sheets off his body, rolls out of bed, and dashes to the window where he finds an ENTOURAGE of black cars speeding down the gravel road, kicking up clouds of gray dust.

INT. FIELD - DAY

With a walkie-talkie gripped in his hand, Marcus -- still dressed in his sleeping clothes -- races across the field as fast as he can...

INT. MASTER BEDROOM, CABIN - DAY

Leon's eyes spring open...

> MARCUS (O.S.)
> Leon! Briana!

Bee wakes next, then Leon rolls out of bed; and as he throws on a pale blue dress shirt and slips into a pair of jeans, Marcus bursts through the door.

> MARCUS (CONT'D)
> (out of breath)
> They found us...

Marcus runs toward the closet -- Leon doesn't bother buttoning the shirt; yet he wears it openly.

With his face pallid, Leon turns to Bee, who, like Leon, is left in a state of shock as well.

> LEON
> No. Please tell me...

> BEE
> (crying)
> He promised me he would leave us alone. I'm so
> sorry, Leon. I didn't mean --

> LUCAS (ON RADIO)
> (screaming)
> Marcus! We're outnumbered! Marcus! Do you
> read me?

Claps of GUNFIRE resonate outside the house, then make their way onto the radio as Lucas screams; however, the claps are delayed and higher in pitch.

> MARCUS (ON RADIO)
> Goddamn it! Get out of there, Lucas!

More screams and gunfire over the walkie-talkie.

EXT. DRIVEWAY - CONTINUOUS

We see the bloody hand of Lucas inching its way toward an Uzi gripped in the hand of another WATCHMAN, dead.

As Lucas -- half of his body riddled with bullets -- crawls closer to the Uzi, a MAN looms over his body.

Lucas fingers the barrel of the Uzi; and as he grabs the handle, the man steps on his hand with a steel toe boot, causing Lucas to yell in agony.

> MARCUS (O.S.)
> Lucas! Get the fuck out of there!

INT. MASTER BEDROOM, CABIN - CONTINUOUS

A gunshot RINGS out over the walkie-talkie!

> BEE
> Leon, I had no idea. Please forgive me --

> LEON
> -- It's not your fault. It's mine.

As Leon rushes to Marcus, Bee grabs Leon from behind. Leon turns around and holds her tightly.

> BEE
> I don't want to lose you, Leon.

Marcus reaches into the closet; rips off a wooden panel. Inside the hidden compartment: a shelf of assault rifles and shotguns. On the floor below: boxes of ammunition.

Leon lets go of Bee and rushes over to Marcus, who passes him a shotgun; however, Leon doesn't grab it.

> MARCUS
> I'll hold them off while you and Bee make it to the treeline. Head directly toward town. I'll meet you behind the Old Diner.

> LEON
> What about you?

> MARCUS
> What about me, Leon?

> LEON
> I'm not going to leave you behind --

Marcus shoves the shotgun into Leon's chest.

> MARCUS
> I'll be right behind you! Now take it! Goddamn it!

Leon grabs the shotgun, then the shells. Loud engines ROAR outside the house, then silence. Marcus leaves the bedroom.

INT. HALLWAY, CABIN - CONTINUOUS

Marcus sees the entourage outside the cabin. There are at least a dozen cars. One GROUP of David's mercenaries flanks the side of the house. Another GROUP flanks the other. The mercenaries, we see, are wearing HELMETS with silver visors.

INT. MASTER BEDROOM, CABIN - CONTINUOUS

Marcus, standing outside the doorway, turns to Leon.

> MARCUS
> Leon! It's either now or never!

INT. HALLWAY, CABIN - CONTINUOUS

Leon cautiously exits the bedroom while Bee stays behind. Marcus turns to Leon, disgusted.

> MARCUS
> (out of breath)
> What the hell are you doing?

> LEON
> I'm not leaving you.

Marcus turns to the front of the cabin, sees the mercenaries flanking the house.

> MARCUS
> Leon, if they catch you, they will torture you!
> They will tear you apart! They will destroy you!
> Is that what you want?

> LEON
> (confidently)
> I'd rather die for something than live for nothing.

Leon pumps the shotgun.

EXT. CABIN - CONTINUOUS

Weapons drawn, mercenaries approach each side of the house.

EXT. DRIVEWAY - CONTINUOUS

A black SUV is parked at the top of a hill. In the back of the SUV, we see David's face through the cracked window.

> DAVID
> (to the radio)
> Remember. I want them alive.

INT. MASTER BEDROOM, CABIN - CONTINUOUS

Bee cowers behind the bed with a handgun gripped in her trembling hands.

INT. LIVING ROOM, CABIN - CONTINUOUS

Marcus and Leon work furiously, overturning whatever they can find such as tables and couches and other pieces of furniture, fortifying themselves in the house.

The first to fire are the mercenaries, who launch a canister of smoke through the living room windows.

As Marcus takes cover behind the overturned couch, he rips off a piece of his shirt and wraps it around the bottom half of his face.

Smokes fills the entire living room; Marcus motions to Leon, unaffected, standing in the midst of the rising smoke.

INT. KITCHEN, CABIN - CONTINUOUS

The kitchen door opens...

Three mercenaries -- now geared with gas masks -- funnel into the kitchen while the living room remains engulfed in smoke. Each mercenary aims his assault rifle at Leon, darting in and out of smoke, only parts of his body seen.

INT. LAUNDRY ROOM, CABIN - CONTINUOUS

With his back against the wall, Marcus closes his eyes and takes in a deep breath.

INT. LIVING ROOM, CABIN - CONTINUOUS

The three mercenaries spread out and stalk through the thick smoke before them.

EXT. CABIN - CONTINUOUS

A shoot-out escalates from inside the house.

INT./EXT. SUV - CONTINUOUS

David motions to the AGENT in the driver's seat.

> DAVID
> I said, 'I want them alive!'

INT. LIVING ROOM, CABIN - CONTINUOUS

Leon stands over the two mercenaries on the ground, the other one lies a couple of feet away from the laundry room. Shot in the back. Leon nods at Marcus standing at the edge of the laundry room. Then Marcus nods back, thanking Leon.

A throbbing sound, as faint as a pulse, steadily builds over the sky above, trembling the foundation of the cabin!

> MARCUS
> What's that sound?

Both Leon and Marcus direct their attention above. A couple of THUDS come from the roof above...

> LEON
> Bee...

EXT. CABIN - CONTINUOUS

The rest of the Aerodyne AGENTS repel from the helicopter to the roof.

INT. MASTER BEDROOM, CABIN - CONTINUOUS

Bee stands to her crouched position and directs her attention to the same THUDS coming from the ceiling.

Suddenly, an AGENT crashes through the window, releases the rope from the harness, and grabs Bee before she can fire a gunshot. Another AGENT crashes through the window, glass shattering everywhere.

> BEE
> Leon! Help!

INT. LIVING ROOM, CABIN - CONTINUOUS

Leon hears screams coming from upstairs.

> LEON
>> Bee...

INT. MASTER BEDROOM, CABIN - CONTINUOUS

Bee kicks and screams and tries to free herself from the agent's grip. The agent knocks the gun from Bee's hand and PUNCHES her across the face, dazing her.

> LEON (O.S.)
>> Bee!

INT. HALLWAY, CABIN - CONTINUOUS

As Leon races down the hallway, another GROUP of mercenaries storm the side of the house. Gunfire blares throughout the house, Marcus firing most of the gunshots below. Leon leans over the banister and witnesses Marcus backpedaling into the living room.

> LEON
> (seething)
>> Marcus!

Two mercenaries shoot Marcus in the kneecaps, causing him to flail to the floor. Marcus, now weaponless, crawls away. Rolls his eyes toward Leon and mouths, "Go."

As the mercenaries drag Marcus from the house, Leon checks on Bee.

INT. MASTER BEDROOM, CABIN - CONTINUOUS

When Leon arrives, Bee is nowhere is sight. Two broken windows, Leon sees, the floor covered in shards of glass. No Bee. Leon lowers his head. Curls his hands into fists.

We stay in front of Leon, his fists trembling in rage, as a TEAM OF AGENTS enter the bedroom in SLOW MOTION.

One agent after another floods through the doorway. As they circle Leon, Leon doesn't raise his head. Doesn't do anything, for that matter. He stands there in the middle of the room -- his body now trembling.

INT. CLOSET, MASTER BEDROOM - CONTINUOUS

With one hand, the agent presses the barrel against Bee's temple. His other hand is held tightly against Bee's mouth.

INT. MASTER BEDROOM, CABIN - CONTINUOUS

The agent makes the first move toward Leon's right hand; however, we still don't see Leon's face, which is directed toward the floor. His body still trembling, as well.

While the other agents keep their guns on Leon, the agent grabs his wrist. Leon rotates around; and that's when we see Leon's monstrous face. Beyond recognizable, his face is. Eyes covered in white. Dark veins stretch across the corners of his eyes like crow's feet. His skin is pale and sickly.

With his other hand, Leon flips the visor from the agent's helmet and gazes directly into the agent's eyes. The agent's face turns to stone.

Two agents leap at Leon; however, Leon is too fast. Whatever life crosses his range of vision turns to stone. He takes out the first three agents without even using the gaze; borrows their own guns. Shoots them dead.

Leon grabs a knife from the agent's holster and goes to town on the other agents. Takes out six agents with close quarter combat, flipping off all of the agents' helmets, gazing them during half strides, their bodies frozen in action poses. Some dead. Some left in a state of paralysis, others drop to the floor from their heavy limbs.

With the team of agents now incapacitated, Leon searches the room for Bee.

A gunshot ECHOES outside...

INT. HALLWAY, CABIN - CONTINUOUS

Leon stands behind the banister. Looks through the front window. In the front of the cabin, Leon sees -- both eyes still as white as marbles -- David standing behind an injured Marcus. He's wearing a visor too. Marcus is not...

> DAVID
> (on megaphone)
> Surrender now or your friend dies! I'm giving you
> to the count of ten! Ten, nine, eight...

EXT. CABIN - CONTINUOUS

David presses the barrel to the back of Marcus's head.

> DAVID (O.S.)
> ...Seven, six, five...

INT. HALLWAY, CABIN - CONTINUOUS

As Marcus raises his head toward the house, Leon closes his eyes and turns away.

> MARCUS (O.S.)
> Don't give in, Leon!

EXT. CABIN - CONTINUOUS

David cocks the hammer of the gun.

> DAVID
> Ah! The hell with this...

> MARCUS
> You gotta fight these motherfuckers with every --

INT. HALLWAY, CABIN - CONTINUOUS

A gunshot suddenly RINGS out!

Leon's eyes open -- still white. He looks ahead and witnesses Marcus on the ground; and he's not moving.

As Leon tightens his jaw with rage, the butt of a pistol comes flying across the backside of Leon's head. POW! Leon runs his hand across the backside of his head. Moves his hand -- now bloody -- in front of his face. His eyes roll into the back of his head. He falls to the floor. And all we see is utter darkness...

BLACK SCREEN

We hear the sound of a woman moaning.

EXT. CABIN - DAY

The darkness gives way to bright sunlight. We see Leon opening his bloodshot eyes, slowly at first. Strings of dried blood caked across his forehead. He's sitting on his knees. Hands tied behind his back. Still dazed.

The AGENT tosses the black bag on the ground. Leon turns to the bag, then to the shadowy agent towering above him.

With his hand, Leon shields his eyes from the sunlight beaming through the overcast sky. He blinks away the blur from his eyes. Looks around. Other agents, he sees, circled around him. Standing stoically. Assault rifles in hands.

Leon draws his eyes before him. Bee, he sees, also kneeled on the ground. Fully aware. Bound by the wrists. Gagged as well. She has a welt on her face. And she's crying.

                    DAVID (O.S.)
        I'm glad you finally decided to join us, Leon.

Two agents break from the circle; David shoulders his way into the circle. He's wearing contacts, which appear like dim sunglasses; however, his iris is slightly visible.

                    DAVID (CONT'D)
                (prowling around Leon)
        You see a ringleader has only two ways to tame a
        lion, with discipline...
                    (MORE)

119

                    DAVID (CONT'D)
          (holding out index finger)
    ...or dominance.
          (then middle finger)
    The first may not be the best way -- effective,
    maybe. If there's one thing about lions, it's their
    predictability.

David kneels down in front of Leon.

                    DAVID (CONT'D)
    You like the new wear? I had them custom
    made. But enough about me, Leo. I know
    you're a man who likes to get down to business.

David stands, nods at AGENT STAMMER, who pulls his hand behind his back, revealing a metal instrument similar to WIRE SPECULUMS.

Two agents grab Leon by the shoulders and keep him from moving. Leon resists, but the pressure applied is too great.

                    DAVID (O.S.) (CONT'D)
    Resistance is a fruitless endeavor.

David steps aside while Agent Stammer places the instrument across Leon's face. Inserts the ends into the corner of Leon's eyelids, which keep them held open.

Bee tries to mumble something underneath the gag, something like, "You son of a bitch!" She struggles as well, but two agents hold her down as well.

David kneels back down to Leon, now eye level.

                    DAVID (CONT'D)
          (turning to Bee)
    You failed to see the mole in your own garden.

Leon spits in David's face; David wipes away the spit with his black tie. Nods to another AGENT. The agent brandishes a cattle prod. Shocks Leon in the back. Leon tenses up.

                    DAVID (CONT'D)
          Again!

The agent shocks Leon once more. Bee attempts to look away; however, the agents force her to look into Leon's eyes.

> DAVID (CONT'D)
> Again! Damn it!

The agent shocks Leon. He takes it. Holds the gaze as long as he can. David, now furious, pulls out a gun and shoots the agent in the head. Removes the cattle prod from the agent's hand and shocks Leon repeatedly.

> DAVID (CONT'D)
> Come on, Leon! Bring out the bitch!

Trembling, Leon lowers his red face, veins swell over his forehead.

> DAVID (CONT'D)
> There she is...

David continues to shock Leon until he gives in...

Leon's head snaps upward, his eyes filled with white, dark veins spreading out from his eyes. Parts of his skin are scaly. He screams, deafening; then the word...

> LEON
> No!

The tears roll down Bee's now gray cheeks, her entire body turns to stone, starting from her face to her feet. Yet, the clothes remain dangling from her stoned body. Leon turns his gaze toward the agents, then David, but it has no effect.

Leon convulses now, his face darkening, then cracking...

Before the gaze takes hold of him completely, the butt of a pistol swings behind Leon's head. POW! Leon flops to the ground. Blacks out. Again...

David hands the gun to the agent.

> DAVID
> (nodding at agent)
> Bag them.

As David walks away, several agents place a black bag over Leon's head and drag his lifeless body toward the armored vehicle.

INT. OPERATING THEATRE, AERODYNE - DAY

In the center of the stage sits an unconscious Leon, hands bound on the arms of the metal chair, black bag still over his head.

The SQUEAK of the door echoes throughout the theatre, revealing the grandness all around. Leon stirs, his head swaying back and forth.

We see the back of David as he strolls toward Leon. The seats in the theatre are empty as well. Only David and Leon.

David stands to the right of Leon, scans his body.

> DAVID
> Welcome home, Leon...

Leon raises his head, fully now. He tries to free himself.

> DAVID (CONT'D)
> ...As I said earlier, resistance is a fruitless
> endeavor.
> > (pacing around Leon)
> Alfred Tennyson once wrote: 'Tis better to have
> loved and lost than never to have loved at all.'

David shakes his head in disgust, then leans in closer.

> DAVID (CONT'D)
> I believe what Mr. Tennyson truly meant to say:
> 'Tis better not to have loved than to have loved at
> all. Love blinds a man, as it did you...

David wags his finger, grins.

> DAVID (CONT'D)
> Who would've thought? This whole time, Leon,
> all you needed was a little TLC. We could've
> simply let you and Bee continue to play house. I
> won't question your intelligence.
> (MORE)

> DAVID (CONT'D)
> I'm sure sooner or later you would've finally
> opened your eyes. But why toss a rare piece of
> meat to the dogs?

David stands behind Leon, places his hand on Leon's shoulder.

> DAVID (CONT'D)
> Don't worry, Leon...
> (in Leon's ear)
> ...the fun has just begun.

EXT. FOREST - DAY

A HUNTER, in his early 60's, and his DOG, a bloodhound, follow the billow of black smoke coming from a ranch.

EXT. CROW'S NEST RANCH - CONTINUOUS

The hunter and his dog stop at the edge of the treeline and witness the aftermath of the shoot-out.

EXT. CABIN - DAY

The dog breaks away from his master and finds Marcus, who is lying on the ground. The dog BARKS! The hunter straps the rifle over his shoulder and hurries to Marcus. Checks the pulse on the side of his neck.

> HUNTER
> Sweet Jesus! Hang in there, buddy.

The hunter reaches his hand in his breast pocket. Pulls out a cell phone. Dials 911.

INT. OPERATING THEATRE, AERODYNE - NIGHT

The metal cuffs around Leon's wrists suddenly spring open from the arms of the chair. Then another door opens, causing Leon to stir. The door is much smaller in size and sound.

Leon removes the bag from his head -- his face, pale and sweaty; eyes, bloodshot. He finds an EXIT door cracked open. Gets up from the chair. Staggers at first, then gathers himself.

INT. HALLWAY, AERODYNE - CONTINUOUS

Leon pokes his head through the door, only to find a deserted hallway. He looks around, confused.

As he steps farther into the hallway, he hears a BEEP to his right. He turns, sees a light flashing over another doorway across the hallway. The light turns from RED to GREEN. The door automatically opens. Leon follows...

INT. ZONE B, AERODYNE - CONTINUOUS

As soon as Leon enters the zone, the door closes behind him. The atmosphere is dimmer, not as bright and white as the previous hallway. Twice the size as well. Leon turns to the large white imprint, "ZONE B," on the concrete wall.

Leon cautiously proceeds down the hallway, which rounds into a circle. Another BEEP, which echoes down the hallway. Leon comes across another door. Above the door, a green light...

As he steps through the door, a surveillance camera above aims its lens on Leon. The light below repeatedly flashes red. He draws his eyes toward the camera. Peers closely.

INT. SURVEILLANCE ROOM, AERODYNE - CONTINUOUS

The guard, TROTTER, 50's, heavyset, rises from the chair. Notices the monitor flashing red. Looks toward the screen.

INT. ZONE B, AERODYNE - CONTINUOUS

Leon's eyes wash over with paleness. Face trembles slightly.

INT. SURVEILLANCE ROOM, AERODYNE - CONTINUOUS

Beads of sweat form over Trotter's forehead. He opens the lid to the ALARM on the console.

As he strikes his palm down on the alarm, his hand suddenly freezes inches away from a red button!

INT. ZONE B, AERODYNE - CONTINUOUS

The light below the camera flashes green. Leon follows...

INT. STORAGE ROOM, AERODYNE - CONTINUOUS

As Leon enters the dimly lit room, the door suddenly closes behind him.

Leon heads directly toward one aisle in particular. He comes across the statue of Tammy. And that's when Leon finally surrenders to his feelings. He falls to his knees and cries.

While sitting in his kneeled position, his eyes cross Tammy's bare gray feet; he runs his fingers across her toes, which are made of coarse stone. His face switches over from great misery to tremendous rage.

Leon rises to his feet, wraps his hands around the statue, and slams it to the ground. The statue shatters into thousands of pieces!

At a distance, we see Leon looming above the broken remains of Tammy.

Once more, he falls to his knees. Picks up a chunk of Tammy's face. Holds it close. His head lowers with both grief and grotesquery.

In the darkness surrounding the small pockets of light, a clatter of footsteps carries over Leon's heavy breath. Leon calms his breathing and hears a man's voice...

MAN'S VOICE

        Leon?

Leon rotates; however, we don't see his face in its entirety, for it remains on the fringe of darkness. The parts we do see partially reveal neither man nor creature.

His skin is scaly. Each strand of his bleached blonde hair softly waggles like the end of a tail, as if the hair is alive in its own way.

Behind him, a MAN steps from the shadows, revealing his scarred face. Leon tilts his head in suspicion.

The scarred-face man, known as "SCARS," steps closer.

>   SCARS
> I'm sure you're starting to feel like a mouse in a
> maze right now. I'm here to guide you to the
> cheese, my friend.

>   LEON
> How can I trust you?

Leon's voice is much deeper and harsher too. Sinister.

>   SCARS
> You trusted Marcus --

Leon turns away.

>   LEON
>   (with his head lowered)
> -- Marcus is dead.

>   SCARS
>   (angrily)
> Zappin?

Leon nods his head. Doesn't answer.

>   SCARS (CONT'D)
> Let's make sure Marcus didn't die for nothing --

>   LEON
> -- I don't need your help.

>   SCARS
> You can't escape here alone. You're going to need
> all the help you can get.

Leon stands to his feet.

                    LEON
              (stepping into the light)
        Whoever said anything about escaping...

Scars takes a step backward.

SERIES OF SHOTS - AERODYNE FORCED ON LOCKDOWN

-- Each light inside Aerodyne's underground facility falls into a momentary blackness, then lights up with red.

-- The alarm RINGS out throughout the corridors of Aerodyne.

-- Guards grab assault rifles and visors from the shelves in the ARMORY.

-- A team of guards form a perimeter around David's office.

INT. DAVID'S OFFICE - CONTINUOUS

David presses a button on the intercom.

                    DAVID
        What the fuck is going on out there?

              GUARD (ON INTERCOM)
        We're on lockdown, sir.

David quickly turns to the monitor next to his desk.

ON THE MONITOR

An empty chair in the operating theatre.

BACK TO DAVID

who frantically switches cameras three times until coming across the feed to the computer room. David clenches his teeth in anger.

Over David's shoulder, we see Leon standing among a wall of flames. As before, we only see a glimpse of Leon...

INT. COMPUTER ROOM, AERODYNE - CONTINUOUS

The sprinklers switch on from the ceiling, but the fire is too great.

Leon stands before a wall of flames while Scars -- who's wearing a standard issued visor -- pushes the rest of the servers to the ground.

Sparks fly and shoot out from the destroyed servers! Scars takes an axe to the guts of the servers, destroys them. Meanwhile...

Leon's white eyes never leaving the flaming GLASS BOX before him. Each side of the box, precisely two feet. At the base of the box is a metal ring. A row of sawtooth blades encompass the interior of the ring.

With keen concentration, Leon focuses on the shark tooth-like blades, then the outlets within the ring. His eyes follow the cords from the base of the box to a conveyer belt which runs into two servers. Destroyed, like the others.

INT. STORAGE ROOM, AERODYNE - NIGHT - FLASHBACK SEQUENCE

Leon and Scars stand in darkness. Scars not making eye contact with Leon's glowing iridescent eyes.

> LEON
> (urgently)
> What's in the box?

> SCARS
> Inside the box holds an idea. As you know, all
> ideas that seem impossible to achieve in our
> lifetime are merely within our grasp in the next.
> Imagine having the power to control every human
> being on this planet through the one thing we rely
> on the most...

Scars pulls out a cell phone from his pocket. Holds it up for Leon to see.

> LEON
> What does it have to do with me?

                          SCARS
                      (looking away)
            It has <u>everything</u> to do with you, Leon.

INT. GALLERY, LEATHERBY MANOR - DAY - FLASHBACK SEQUENCE

Leon, only a young boy, stands in front of the glass case and stares at the Medusa
head inside.

INT. TESTING ROOM C, AERODYNE - DAY - FLASHBACK SEQUENCE

The ASSISTANT ENGINEER measures the dimensions around Leon's neck.

                          LEON
                      (jokingly)
            The last time someone took my measurements
            was when I bought my first suit.

                  ASSISTANT ENGINEER
            Prom?

Leon drifts in thought. Face slackens.

                          LEON
                      (quietly)
            No. Funeral.

The assistant engineer places her hand on Leon's shoulder, smiles.

                  ASSISTANT ENGINEER
            Don't worry, Mr. Dorsey. I guarantee this will be
            much better than a suit.

INT. STORAGE ROOM, AERODYNE - NIGHT - FLASHBACK SEQUENCE

Leon snaps from his trance.

                          LEON
            It must be destroyed.

INT. COMPUTER ROOM, AERODYNE - NIGHT - PRESENT DAY

Leon rips off the metal pipe from a panel and rams the end of it into the top of the box. The glass cracks, barely. Leon strikes yet again. Cracks slither farther across the box.

We see a QUICK FLASH of an image: on the side of a pillow, Bee's face wrapped in moonlight, her eyes glazed with tears.

Leon shakes the image from his mind, rears back, and strikes once more!

CRASH!

The box shatters to bits and pieces...

> SCARS (O.S.)
> Time to leave, Leon!

Leon doesn't budge, his eyes mesmerized by the flames. Scars rushes toward the door. Peeks through the window. Sees armed GUARDS marching down the hallway.

> SCARS (CONT'D)
> Leon! We don't have much time! Let's go!

INT. SURVEILLANCE ROOM, AERODYNE - CONTINUOUS

A GUARD notices Trotter standing motionlessly in front of the wall of monitors -- several monitors displaying a shoot-out on the screen.

> GUARD
> (confusedly)
> Trotter?

The guard turns his eyes toward Trotter's hand hovered over the alarm. His arm remains motionless as well. The guard witnesses the strings of blood caked below each of Trotter's nostrils. His jaw is lowered, mouth gaping, head shaking.

Unable to fully rotate his head, Trotter rolls his eyes toward the guard and moans.

The guard looks down and tries to lift Trotter's hand; however, his arm is completely frozen.

                    GUARD (CONT'D)
        Holy shit.

As the guard rests Trotter's stiff body on the floor, his eyes cross one monitor in particular. The guard's eyes widen in fascination.

ON THE MONITOR

With a stoned head in his hand, Leon prowls toward a pleading GUARD on his knees. The guard's shielding his face with his arm; however, his arm has been turned into stone. Half of it -- forearm to fingertip -- is shattered over the floor. Leon smashes in the guard's face with the head.

BACK TO THE GUARD

who moves his eyes toward other monitors. Each guard in the monitor isn't moving, including a team surrounding the lobby.

The guard looks closer.

ON THE MONITOR

Each guard has been turned to stone.

INT. LOBBY, AERODYNE - CONTINUOUS

Leon kneels down to Scars, who is bleeding out from the bullet hole in his neck. Leon presses his hand against the wound, trying to stop the bleeding.

                    SCARS
        I want to see with my own...
                (gagging)
        ...my...

Scars removes the visor from his face and looks into Leon's eyes; however, we still don't see Leon's face in its entirety.

Panic fills Scars eyes, now fixated; however, he doesn't turn to stone. Why? Scars is already dead.

INT. DAVID'S OFFICE, AERODYNE - NIGHT

David hears a barrage of gunfire behind the locked door. Following the gunfire, screams of terror.

In a state of surrender, David slides to his knees and backs himself against the back of his desk. Covers his ears. Closes his eyes.

A loud THUD resonates through the office!

David's eyes bolt open.

Below the desk, we see Leon's feet walking across the office...

Leon stops next to David's desk. David doesn't turn to Leon. His eyes remain ahead; however, in the corner of his eye, he finds a tall and dark figure looming over his curled body.

DAVID

You honestly think the world will accept you for
<u>what</u> you are...
    (scowling)
...They will pick you apart like vultures -- nibble
by nibble, taking whatever they can for their own
personal gain. Sooner or later, you'll beg them to
kill you. You think you can be civilized, Leon.
What if you're in traffic...
    (out of breath)
...a driver cuts in front of you? What if a
pedestrian accidently bumps shoulders with you?
You have <u>no</u> control over the lion inside of you.
You're a killer. You always will be. Tell me.
What does a lion fear most than death itself,
Leon?

Leon kneels down to David's eye level. David swallows the dry lump down his throat. Keeps his eyes ahead, trying not to look Leon in the eyes.

LEON

My name's not Leon. It's <u>Freeze</u>...

David slowly rolls his eyes toward Leon, his face now only inches away from his.

We finally see Leon's veiny face in its entirety. His skin is much darker, bumpy and yet smooth like a snake. His eyes, all white. No pupil. No iris.

David makes eye contact with Leon. So hard, David clenches, his teeth shatter and crumble from his lips. David moans, quietly at first, then deafening.

David's face stills with his mouth open. His scream fades into a soft gurgle. The rest of his body, including his face, turns into a courtyard statue.

Leon stands upright. Exits. We watch Leon walking away through the smoke from the previous gunfire, as well as the rain coming down from the sprinklers. Never looks back. Only moves forward.

INT. MASTER BEDROOM, LEATHERBY MANOR - DAY

With an old photograph of Peter and young Diego, 15 years old, standing in front of Aztec temple, Diego stands in front of the dresser.

We PULL BACK and see Diego's true self. He is bald. What sticks out the most is the pink SCAR on the left side of his scalp. Below the scar rests a SHUNT buried underneath the skin. Diego doesn't look at the photo with fond memories; instead, he carries nothing but solace from the sight of the photo.

He places the photo on top of the dresser. Opens the top drawer. Pulls out a rusty can of ALTOIDS. Opens can.

Slowly and ever so carefully, he peels back the dusty paper and pulls out one of a dozen or so Medusa scales from the inside. Holds the scale close to his face.

INT. HALLWAY, SAINT MARY MEMORIAL - DAY

We see the back of a well-dressed MAN, cloaked in all black, walking through a set of doors. The sign above the OPEN button reads, "Intensive Care Unit."

The mysterious man in black strolls past both doctors and nurses alike. He ignores the NURSE'S DESK and proceeds directly toward the hospital room.

INT. HOSPITAL ROOM - CONTINUOUS

The man in black stops at the doorway. Removes his black fedora with his left hand. Diego is revealed with a head full of salt and pepper hair.

In the other hand, Diego holds a vase of blue roses. He walks toward the hospital bed where Marcus lies unconscious. He's hooked up to machines, including a ventilator. Wears a fresh white bandage over his forehead.

Diego places the vase on the tray next to Marcus's bed and stands by his bedside.

> DIEGO
> Hang in there, old friend.

Diego gently places his hand on top of Marcus's hand.

INT. CHLOE'S BEDROOM - DAY

We see a a pair of children's hands stacking small colored blocks on top of one another. The child places the blues with the blues. Reds with reds. Yellows with yellows. Makes three stacks. The red being higher than the other colors. A woman's voice from above --

> WOMAN'S VOICE
> Very good, Chloe.

We PULL BACK and see young CHLOE, five years old, dirty blonde hair, looks identical to her anonymous father. She's sitting on the carpet. There's a bed in the room. Pink dresser. Unicorn wallpaper on the wall. Doll house as well.

Chloe carefully scans the building blocks, making sure each one is perfectly stacked.

The woman, we see, DOCTOR DHAWAN, 30's, Indian, attractive, dressed in a white coat, black skirt; mirror-tinted sunglasses dangle from her breast pocket. She picks up the green triangle from the beige carpet.

> DOCTOR DHAWAN
> How about this piece, Chloe?

The doctor hands Chloe the green triangle. Chloe thinks for a moment, then places the triangle on the stack of red blocks.

> DOCTOR DHAWAN (O.S.) (CONT'D)
> Why did you place the triangle on that particular
> piece?

> CHLOE
> (drawling)
> It's a roof to protect all the red people.

> DOCTOR DHAWAN
> (amusingly)
> The red people? I see. And why not place 'the
> roof' on the other blocks?

The only response the doctor receives is a vacant expression.

> DOCTOR DHAWAN (CONT'D)
> Chloe?

Chloe points to the blue blocks.

> CHLOE
> Blue people are sad. Yellow people are scared.
> Red people...

> DOCTOR DHAWAN
> The red people?

> CHLOE
> They're mad.

> DOCTOR DHAWAN
> I see. And why do you want to protect the mad
> people, Chloe?

Chloe bashfully shrugs, lowers her head. As Doctor Dhawan vigilantly rotates her head toward the large mirror on the wall, Chloe tilts her head upward. A tiny iridescent light flickers in the corner of her eye...

INT. OBSERVATIONAL ROOM - CONTINUOUS

On the other side of the mirror stands a crowd of ENGINEERS and
SCIENTISTS. One in particular, dressed in a expensive suit, well-groomed,
ashen face, stands behind the other men, in the shadows. And he's smoking a
cigarette.

> SMOKER
> How much longer until she's ready for trials?

> BRANT
> The software is eighty percent complete.
> However...

The engineer, BRANT, late 20's, beard, glasses, messy hair, points at Chloe
behind the glass.

> BRANT (CONT'D)
> ...the hardware needs a little more time to
> develop. I'm afraid undertaking a project as
> intricate as this one requires a little bit of time
> and patience.

> SMOKER
> Two things that I don't have, Mister --

> BRANT
> Brant, sir.

> SMOKER
> Give me a time line, Mr. Brant.

Brant contemplates, then answers.

> BRANT
> Two years, Mr. President.

The smoker, PRESIDENT LOCKHART, drags from the cigarette. Exhales.
Tosses the cigarette into a coffee cup. The side door opens. At the doorway
stands another man, identical to the CHAUFFEUR, no bullet hole. A twin
perhaps? Or is something far more perfidious?

> CHAUFFEUR
> The car is ready, Mr. President.

LOCKHART
Get it done, Mr. Brant, or else...

Lockhart turns to the chauffeur, points at him, and then glares at Brant.

LOCKHART (CONT'D)
...you'll be replaced.

The President exits the room.

A KNOCK on the door...

INT. GALLERY, LEATHERBY MANOR - NIGHT

The door cracks open. We see the back of Leon, now in his 50's; however, he looks nearly twice his age. Wrinkly skin, weak posture, trembly hands: traits associated with a man ready to turn up his toes.

At the doorway stands Diego, much older but still <u>remarkably</u> fit for his age.

DIEGO
Am I interrupting, sir?

With a snake-handle cane in his hand, Leon slouches in front of the case. Inside perches the same decrepit head as before. Still intact. Part of Medusa's face is missing. Most of the scales, gone.

LEON
What is it, Diego?

DIEGO
We found her, sir.

LEON
How sure are you?

DIEGO
A hundred percent.

We move closer toward Leon; however, his back is still facing us.

LEON
Contact, Marcus. Tell him that they'll be looking for her.

DIEGO
(uncertainly)
Pardon, sir. Who will be looking for her?

LEON
Everyone.

We CLOSE IN on the glass case and see the reflection of Leon's eyes; and at that very moment, we discover that Leon has <u>no</u> eyes. All that remains is scar tissue from where Leon ripped out his eyes with his bare hands.

FADE TO BLACK.

HERE IS AN EXCLUSIVE
FIRST LOOK AT THE SEQUEL...

Hard Pressed

BLACK SCREEN

We hear the rotary blades of a police helicopter pulsating through a night sky.

> ANNE (V.O.)
> I find myself wondering why he did it -- why he
> killed all those people. Then I think about what
> they did to him. I would've done the same thing.
> That's the truth...

FADE IN:

INT. LIVING ROOM, LEON'S CONDO - NIGHT

The flickering spotlight flickers through the windows, highlighting sections of the luxurious room: high ceilings, white leather furniture, polished glass tables, chandeliers.

On a leather chair rests a injured security GUARD, blonde hair, now stained red with blood, tall and handsome, curled in severe anguish. His face is dressed with fresh bruises. Strings of blood dribble from the corners of his mouth, ruining the white leather underneath.

A guttural scream of horror JOLTS the guard from his drifting state and forces him to turn toward the bathroom...

INT. BATHROOM, LEON'S CONDO - CONTINUOUS

A bloody tooth dances in the sink, the plug preventing it from falling down into the drain. Three other teeth remain inside the stopped sink, all bloody.

In front of the sink stands Leon, now 37 years old; however, we don't see his face, only from the chin down -- and he too is bleeding from the mouth. His hands are dripping with fresh blood as well. His knuckles, flecked with cuts and loose skin in the shape of snake scales.

Leon spits out a dark clot of blood into the sink.

We see Leon from behind: tall and handsome, bleached blonde hair, similar profile as the guard.

INT. LIVING ROOM, LEON'S CONDO - NIGHT

Leon walks toward the guard, causing him to moan in agony.

> COP (V.O.)
> You're completely surrounded, Freeze! Come out
> with hands up!

Leon grabs the guard by the arm; however, the guard recoils.

> GUARD
> Please...

A rope of blood pours from the guard's mouth, his mouth without any teeth whatsoever...

Leon backslaps the guard, forcing him back into an unconscious state.

INT. UPTOWN CONDOMINIUMS - CONTINUOUS

A group of SWAT AGENTS huddle around the front entrance of the building, a swarm of red and blue lights from sirens flashing all around them like an Italian disco.

One of the agents, DOPPLER, cocks the assault rifle.

> DOPPLER
> Shoot to kill.

Doppler slides down the helmet's tinted visor over his eyes, then the other SWAT AGENTS follow suit and shield their eyes.

INT. LIVING ROOM, LEON'S CONDO - CONTINUOUS

Leon grabs the hammer from the table. Walks to the guard.

> LEON
> This may sting a bit...

INT. FIRST FLOOR, UPTOWN CONDOMINIUMS - CONTINUOUS

The agents methodically spread out like veins, one line of agents funneling up one staircase while other line of agents heading toward the lobby.

INT. LIVING ROOM, LEON'S CONDO - CONTINUOUS

As the spotlight flickers all around Leon, he rises from the guard's lifeless body. Then rushes from the room.

INT. FOYER, LEON'S CONDO - CONTINUOUS

The front door opens...

Leon peeks through the crack; and along the distant walls, he sees growing shadows, as lanky as stick figures. He closes the door, carefully. Ducks back into the condo.

INT. KITCHEN, LEON'S CONDO - CONTINUOUS

Leon dumps a gallon of bleach over the bloody hammer. Tosses it back into the drawer. Hurries to the black duffel on the counter, which is left partially open.

Inside the bag: a change of clothes, a stainless steel pistol with a wooden grip, a wrinkled photo of a young girl no older than five years old; and, lastly, a strange black device in the shape of a magazine clip.

After he zips the bag close, he prowls from the kitchen -- the pale spotlight flickering behind him like a strobe light; however, the light remains behind him, keeping both his face and body masked in utter darkness.

INT. HALLWAY, THIRTY-SIXTH FLOOR - CONTINUOUS

At least fifty agents line each side of the wall. Guns drawn. Ready to "Shoot to kill."

One agent in particular, POWELL, younger, stands with both his legs and hands trembling.

The agent next to him, TUCKET, or "TUCK," much older, nods at Powell.

TUCKET
Remember, kid. Don't look directly in his eyes.

In return, Powell bobs his head. Tightens his grip around the assault rifle. He's as ready as he'll ever be.

INT. FOYER, LEON'S CONDO - CONTINUOUS

Two gunshots RING out!

The hinges of the front door rip in half from the gunshot; then, immediately after, an agent knocks down the door with the blunt side of a sledgehammer!

As the door flings open, the group of agents stream into the condo, still coming in and out of light from the helicopter hovering outside. Guns drawn. Ready...

AGENT (O.S.)
Clear!

INT. LIVING ROOM, LEON'S CONDO - CONTINUOUS

The agents come across a body on the ground, the guard.

AGENT #3 (O.S.)
Kitchen! Clear!

AGENT #1 kneels down and checks the guard's pulse along the side of his neck.

AGENT #2
Is he alive?

AGENT #2 stands guard, looking around in paranoia.

AGENT #1
Barely.

While the other agents check the remainder of the condo, the Agent #2 directs his attention toward the teeth scattered along the floor.

A couple of teeth remain inside the guard's gaping mouth; however, the teeth do not belong to the guard...

                    AGENT #2
            Where's the rest of his teeth?

INT. GUEST BEDROOM, LEON'S CONDO - CONTINUOUS

As Powell takes a step through the doorway, Agent Tucket creeps from behind. Wraps his arm around Powell's neck. Squeezes tightly.

                    TUCKET
                  (whispering)
            Drop the gun...

Powell hesitates. Doesn't drop the gun at first.

                TUCKET (CONT'D)
                  (sharply)
            ...Now!

Tucket presses the barrel of the gun against the side of Powell's head to let him know he means business.

Powell finally drops the gun to the floor, then Tucket guides him farther into the dark bedroom.

INT. BATHROOM, LEON'S CONDO - CONTINUOUS

Agent #2 finds blood splattered over the sink.

                    AGENT #2
            Something's not right...

INT. GUEST BEDROOM, LEON'S CONDO - CONTINUOUS

As Tucket steps forward into a beam of dim light cast from the window, we see Tucket's visor. The left side of the visor is badly cracked, only exposing his left eye.

In the corner of the bedroom, the spotlight from outside the window flickers over a DARK FIGURE standing against the wall.

We see the figure's keen white eyes, held like knives along Tucket's eye -- the left one -- then the blood caked over the corner of his mouth. It's Leon! And he's gazing Tucket; however, Tucket has <u>not</u> turned to stone...

INT. LIVING ROOM, LEON'S CONDO - NIGHT

With his head held downward in a lifeless state, Tucket staggers from the GUEST BEDROOM and manages to find his way to the other agents.

> AGENT #1
> Tucket?

A large amount of blood gushes from Tucket's helmet; then, Tucket stumbles and eventually falls to the floor.

> AGENT #2
> He's here...

While Agent #1 tends to Tucket, the other agents follow the trail of blood to the guest bedroom.

INT. HALLWAY, THIRTY-SIXTH FLOOR - CONTINUOUS

A LONE AGENT, dressed as a member of the SWAT team, prowls past other agents, acknowledging them with a subtle nod.

INT. GUEST BEDROOM, LEON'S CONDO - CONTINUOUS

The agents follow the trail of blood on the floor. The trail leads to a lit bathroom.

INT. ELEVATOR, UPTOWN CONDOMINIUMS - CONTINUOUS

As the elevator doors close, the lone agent switches on the EMERGENCY STOP button and then unzips the duffel bag.

Empties the contents from inside, starting with the change of clothes, the gun, the photo, then the DETONATOR, which he places gently on the floor.

INT. HALLWAY, THIRTY-SIXTH FLOOR - CONTINUOUS

An agent draws his attention toward the elevator light above. Cautiously strolls to the elevator.

INT. ELEVATOR, UPTOWN CONDOMINIUMS - CONTINUOUS

The lone agent kicks open a compartment on the panel below the level buttons. Stuffs the duffel bag inside.

Next, the lone agent inserts the folded clothes underneath his vest. Holsters the gun. Pockets the photo.

INT. HALLWAY, THIRTY-SIXTH FLOOR - CONTINUOUS

As the agent presses the DOWN arrow, the elevator descends to the FIRST FLOOR.

INT. GUEST BATHROOM, LEON'S CONDO - CONTINUOUS

As the agents arrive at the bathroom, they find Powell, unconscious, dressed in a white undershirt and a pair of undies, seated on the toilet.

INT. ELEVATOR, UPTOWN CONDOMINIUMS - CONTINUOUS

The number on the panel counts down: THIRD FLOOR, SECOND FLOOR, FIRST FLOOR...

The lone agent opens the detonator. Presses the red button on top of the detonator.

INT. GUEST BATHROOM, LEON'S CONDO - CONTINUOUS

The agent grabs the radio on his shoulder.

> AGENT (ON RADIO)
> He's dressed like an agent! I repeat, 'Freeze is --

EXT. UPTOWN CONDOMINIUMS - CONTINUOUS

A massive explosion rips through Leon's condo and the entire rooftop above!

EXT. MARKET STREET, UPTOWN - CONTINUOUS

In awe, POLICE OFFICERS, as well as SPECTATORS waiting behind the barricade, watch the giant ball of flames erupt from the top floors of the high-rise condominiums.

A couple of officers instruct spectators to move farther back, warning them of any debris that may rain down from the explosion.

INT. MAIN LOBBY - CONTINUOUS

The elevator doors open with a distorted DING; then the lone agent stumbles from the elevator.

A young police officer, OFFICER GALLOP, who stands guard outside the revolving doors turns toward the elevator, then rushes toward the lone agent.

> OFFICER GALLOP
> Are you injured, sir?

The lone agent bobs his head. Grabs his ribs.

Officer Gallop attempts to remove the lone agent's helmet, but the lone agent groans and grabs the officer's hand and tightly squeezes.

> OFFICER GALLOP (CONT'D)
> Sorry, sir...

The officer wraps his arm around the lone agent, helps him from the building.

EXT. UPTOWN CONDOMINIUMS - CONTINUOUS

Both Officer Gallop and the lone agent rush from the building as the flames
ROAR above -- the officer doing his best to keep the lone agent from stumbling to
the ground.

EXT. MARKET STREET, UPTOWN - CONTINUOUS

Officer Gallop rushes the lone agent to the two PARAMEDICS perched outside an
ambulance. All three of them, including the officer, sit the lone agent in the back
of the ambulance.

                         LONE AGENT
                Thanks, kid...

The officer nods, then rushes back to the condominiums, while one paramedic
checks the lone agent's injuries -- the other one stepping into the back of the
ambulance.

The lone agent keeps on the helmet as a glob of blood trickles from his mouth.

The paramedic takes note of this, as well as the lone agent's labored breathing.

INT. AMBULANCE - CONTINUOUS

The paramedic steps into the ambulance.

                         PARAMEDIC
                    (to the other paramedic)
                I need some gauzes...

The other paramedic searches through a compartment for gauzes.

                      PARAMEDIC (CONT'D)
                ...and a cuff.

The paramedic rotates back around, only to find an empty ambulance. No
SWAT agent.

The paramedic hurries outside, searching for the agent through the dense crowd.
The agent is nowhere to be found...

149

PARAMEDIC (CONT'D)
Where the hell did he go?

EXT. ALLEYWAY, FIFTH STREET - CONTINUOUS

The lone agent dumps the SWAT gear in the dumpster. Keeps the gun, the photo, as well as the change of clothes.

INT. MAIN LOBBY, UPTOWN CONDOMINIUMS - CONTINUOUS

Two FBI AGENTS, both dressed in expensive suits, not gear, are greeted by LIEUTENANT RANDOLPH, 60's, male; however, we do not see the FBI agents' faces, just their nice suits.

FBI AGENT #1
Any survivors?

RANDOLPH
There's nothing left up there. The entire floor
was completely destroyed --

FBI AGENT #1
-- I want the body.

RANDOLPH
But half of my men are gone!

AGENT #1
Do whatever it takes, Lieutenant.

Randolph hesitates to answer. A tense silence.

RANDOLPH
(finally)
Yes, sir.

EXT. ROOFTOP - NIGHT

Standing behind the ledge is Leon, or FREEZE. Heavily breathing. He watches the flames rise before him, a thick black cloud of smoke curling into the night sky, masking the brilliant moon.

Then, we finally see Leon's face in its entirety: a rugged face, handsome, blue eyes, fire breathing inside those eyes, two lines running like valleys between his brows, the rage worn like a mask on his face.

INT. THE MASTER'S BEDROOM, LEATHERBY MANOR - DAY

Leon wakes with a loud grunt; however, we don't see his face in its entirety, only his aged chin and below.

As Leon grabs the side of his face in agony -- occasionally stretching his jaw -- he sits upright with another loud grunt, this time louder and filled with incredible ache.

> SOPHIA (O.S.)
> Mr. Dorsey? Is everything okay?

At the doorway stands Leon's nurse, SOPHIA, early 30's, Latino, beautiful, well-fit, dressed in greenish blue scrubs.

Leon sits on the edge of the bed, his back facing us as the sun shines through the open curtains. He's slumped like an old, sickly man well into his late 80's.

INT. KITCHEN, LEATHERBY MANOR - CONTINUOUS

As Leon's butler, DIEGO TOVAR, fitted in the classical attire, places the cup of tea on the tray, he directs his attention to a couple of THUDS coming from upstairs.

INT. HALLWAY, LEATHERBY MANOR - DAY

With a tray in hand, Diego walks stoically toward the MASTER'S BEDROOM where Sophia is standing with her arms crossed outside the room.

> DIEGO (O.S.)
> What seems to be the problem?

> SOPHIA
> He's getting worse...

> DIEGO
> Jasmine needs a hand downstairs.

Sophia throws her arms downward. Storms away.

INT. THE MASTER'S BEDROOM, LEATHERBY MANOR - CONTINUOUS

Diego steps into the bedroom, only to find a medical tray, a glass, a medicine bottle, and pills scattered in a puddle of water on the floor.

> DIEGO
> Master Dorsey?

Leon, still seated along the edge of the bed, holds his head downward. Sniffles up loose phlegm.

> LEON
> Do whatever it takes, Diego.

Diego places the tray with the tea on the dresser and walks farther into the bedroom.

> DIEGO
> But sir, what if she --

> LEON
> -- I don't care how you do it! Just do it goddamn it! I'm running...

Leon suddenly coughs violently.

Diego sighs, carefully and quietly. Looks at the aging man with steady, unblinking eyes.

> DIEGO
> As you wish.

INT. DRUG STORE - NIGHT

Standing with a weakened posture is STEVEN PRICE, 20's, white, bundled up in a red fleece.

Steven coughs into his hand as he reaches for the bottle of NYQUIL on the shelf. Reads the back, briefly.

EXT. SIDEWALK, PARK ROAD - NIGHT

The street is quiet, except for the wind howling through the bright night. Only a few cars on the road.

As Steven walks with the pharmacy bag in his hand, he turns his shoulder, only to find a strange car, disguised with the night, no headlights, slowing down as it approaches him.

The car inches behind Steven, as he quickens his pace toward his own car, a gold 2012 MAXIMA, parked along the street.

As Steven steps from the curb, the car -- now visible as the streetlight cast its faint amber light from above -- stops beside the Maxima. He shoots a glance at the car, a black LINCOLN, older model, then scurries around the Maxima.

A strange MAN whistles from the passenger seat; however, his face is covered in the shadows.

> MAN
> (from the passenger seat)
> Hey, Stevie!

Steven draws his attention upward at the dark figure inside the Lincoln...

A gunshot suddenly rings out, hitting Steven in the chest!

The blast of the shotgun violently sends him backwards!

He falls to the sidewalk, crawls away. The man steps out of the Lincoln, strolls up to Steven, now choking on his own blood.

Steven holds out his hand in surrender.

> STEVEN
> Ple...ease...

The man -- his face disguised with a BLACK BALACLAVA -- aims the shotgun at Steven's face and finishes him off with another gunshot.

Before the man strolls away, he reaches into the inner pocket of his jacket, pulls out a BLUE ROSE, and tosses it on Steven's dead body.

INT. BEDROOM, ANNE'S FOSTER HOME - DREAM

A lanky man, LOUIS, 40's, unbuckles his belt as he creeps into the bedroom. Stops in front of a juvenile's bed. His head lowers to the floor.

IN THE CLOSET

A young girl gasps, then tightly shuts her eyes.

Louis's head jerks toward the closet. His eyes move spasmodically, as if they're speaking in their own alien way. He follows with a crooked smile on his face.

> LOUIS (O.S.)
> (lecherously)
> What are we going to do with you?

The girl, young ANNE, twelve years old, listens closely to the sound of leather cracking as Louis inches closer...

A SQUEAK of a door!

Her heavy eyes bolt open...

Two headlights, Anne sees, racing toward her at a blinding speed.

INT. ANNE'S BEDROOM - DAY - PRESENT DAY

We PULL BACK from ANNE, much older now, 24 years old, who wakes with a gasp. Her hair is damp and matted, much darker too, eyes bloodshot, wears nightly pajamas: a pair of black undies with a gray tanktop.

Anne pulls her head from the pillow and checks the door, which is opened.

A black long haired cat, EDDIE, short for Edgar Allan Poe, leaps onto the bed, causing Anne to flinch.

> ANNE
> Eddie! You scared me!

Anne strokes the top of Eddie's head, causing the cat to purr. She turns to the clock on the nightstand. The time switches from 6:59 to 7:00.

As the alarm goes off, Anne strikes the SNOOZE button. Rolls out of bed first, then rolls her eyes toward the black and white painting on the wall: a long, narrow weathered dock stretching out into a foggy lake.

INT. ANNE'S BATHROOM - CONTINUOUS

Anne grabs a case of contacts from the medicine cabinet and inserts each contact into her eyes. Rapidly blinks.

Next, as Anne stands in front of the mirror, she opens the drawer and grabs a pink comb. She primps, then pats down the remaining rogue hairs with a sheet of fabric softener.

Lastly, Anne gazes into the reflection of her eyes in the mirror. Turns away before she can get lost in them.

INT. GARAGE - DAY

With a thermos in her hand and a leather purse, as old and chapped as winter lips, worn over her shoulder, Anne steps from the doorway.

Her attire is somewhat modest: a blue blouse worn underneath a black sweater, black pants, very little makeup, only a shade of dark shadow, a dash of powder on her sunken cheeks to cover up the dim freckles, a generous amount of mascara, glossy pink lipstick.

Anne fumbles for the keys, locks the door behind her, then hurries to the white Honda Civic -- an older model -- which is already being warmed up.

As Anne opens the door, she draws her attention toward the unmarked van parked across the street. She spots a ROOFER on top of the house who stops what he's doing and carefully draws his attention toward Anne.

INT. ANNE'S HONDA CIVIC - DAY

As Anne makes a right from her neighborhood, she shoots a glance in the rear view mirror.

Not too far behind her: a suspicious black Lincoln. Two men dressed in black inside. Black shades. Sketchy.

INT. ANNE'S HONDA CIVIC - DAY

Morning traffic at its worst. Anne lets out a sigh. She removes her hand from the steering wheel, holds it to her face. Her hand, now trembling.

Frantically, Anne looks to her left and witnesses the man in the car beside her laughing hysterically, and then the woman on the other side chatting to what looks like herself.

Her face suddenly turns pallid, sweat beads form around her forehead. Throat tightens. She takes in deep belly breaths.

Before the panic can take hold, she switches on the radio, turns the station to 93.7 THE CRUISE; the song "WHITE RABBIT" by Jefferson Airplane is playing. Anne calms.

EXT. PARKING LOT - DAY

Anne pulls into the open parking space underneath a maple tree.

INT. ANNE'S HONDA CIVIC - CONTINUOUS

Anne does one last primp before exiting the car; then, she pulls out a medicine bottle from her purse and downs the drug, PAXIL, with the rest of the coffee from the thermos.

INT. ELEVATOR, CORPORATE BUILDING - DAY

As Anne rides the elevator to the fifth floor, USR, Universal Satellite Radio, she takes in a deep breath through her nose and exhales through her mouth.

INT. OFFICE, USR - DAY

Anne walks to the break room.

INT. BREAK ROOM, USR - CONTINUOUS

Anne enters her social security number in the clock-in device on the wall.

INT. OFFICE, USR - DAY

As Anne makes her way toward her cubicle, she makes eye contact with her coworker and friend, JAMIE VASQUEZ, 30's, slender frame, healthy-looking face, short curly hair with orange highlights, wears lots of jewelry, mainly bracelets.

Jamie covers the microphone from her telephone headset.

> JAMIE
> Hello there, Stranger! So, how was your
> weekend?

Anne stops at the cubicle, leans over.

> ANNE
> (casually)
> Oh! I can't complain. And you?

> JAMIE
> Did you get that photo I sent you?

> ANNE
> I did. Must be nice having a friend with a lake
> house.

A smile from Anne; then she walks away.

> JAMIE
> Hey! I can't complain...

> ANNE
> (over her shoulder)
> Lucky.

Anne laughs, then Jamie follows suit.

About ten cubicles down is Anne's cubicle. She gives a nod of "Hello" to her coworker, STAN, mid 30's, patchy beard, already making a sale in the cubicle next to hers while trying to solve a Rubik's cube in his hands.

Stan nods back, mouths, "Good morning," as Anne can't help but draw her attention toward the Rubik's cube.

INT. ANNE'S CUBICLE, USR - CONTINUOUS

Anne places her purse on the desk and sits down in the chair, checks her personal calendar for the month of OCTOBER, the week of Monday, the 20th, skims through Monday and Tuesday.

INSERT - THE CALENDAR, which reads:

> "Monday, cardio @ 5:30, Necklace!!! 'THE END
> ZONE' @ 9; Tuesday, Pick Up Dry Cleaners @
> 1:00, workout, Doctor's Apt. @ 3:45, 'BLOOD
> DIARIES' @ 10."

BACK IN THE CUBICLE

The desk is covered with various knickknacks: a Teddy bear holding a cup of pens and pencils; a giant smiley face button that says, "HAVE A NICE DAY;" a couple of Happy Meal toys all stationed in tactical positions; and a couple of clippings from the comic, DILBERT, tacked on the walls of her cubicle.

Anne awakens the computer, then types on the keyboard.

ON THE MONITOR

> To the right of ID, words appear on the bar:

> "ANNE ROTH."

> Underneath ID, and to the right of the word PASSWORD, Anne types,
> "ALCATRAZ123."

BACK TO ANNE

who hovers the cursor over the red KOI CARP icon called GO FISH on the dock.

ON THE MONITOR

The Internet application opens, then Anne's homepage, MY HOROSCOPE.

BACK TO ANNE

who scrolls down the website's page until she comes across her zodiac sign, AQUARIUS.

> ANNE
> (reading)
> Be on the lookout. You have a secret admirer.
> (trailing off)
> Yeah right...

A CLICKING sound of a pen being opened and closed, opened and closed, pulls Anne's attention from the computer screen.

Anne turns her shoulder, slowly, only to find her supervisor, DAVE FULLER, six feet five inches tall, slender frame but a bag for a belly, clipboard in hand as well, stalking closer.

As Dave approaches, Anne checks the clock, which reads, "9:11," then places the headset over her head.

INT. DISCOVERY ZONE - DAY

Anne sits in front of the aquarium of jellyish. On her lap is a half-eaten peanut butter and jelly sandwich on top of a crushed brown bag. Next to her is a newspaper, opened to the OBITUARY section. We see one name in particular, Steven Price.

After Anne pulls her eyes away from Steven's picture, she turns toward the glowing jellyfish floating gracefully through the water.

INT. ANNE'S CUBICLE, USR - DAY

Anne remains on her headset, her worn eyes attached to a list of costumers displayed on the monitor before her.

> ANNE
> Hello, may I speak to Ms. Corset?

                    MS. CORSET (V.O.)
Who's calling?

                    ANNE
My name is Anne Roth, and I'm calling from
Universal Satellite Radio. How are you doing
today, Ms. Corset?

                    MS. CORSET (V.O.)
                    (impatiently)
Fine.

                    ANNE
Wonderful. The reason I'm calling you today is
that we've noticed that you canceled your
subscription to Universal Satellite Radio and, at
this time, we would like to offer you a special six
month package for --

Heavy breathing on the other end of the line, Anne listens closely.

                    MS. CORSET (V.O.)
-- Why are you doing this to me?

We see a snake, a BOA CONSTRICTOR, slithering from underneath Anne's
cubicle.

                    ANNE
                    (hesitantly)
Well, we here at USR have enjoyed your business,
Ms. Corset, and would love to have you back as a
customer.

The snake slithers around Anne's foot, smelling Anne's flesh with its tongue.

                    MS. CORSET (V.O.)
You listen to me, you bitch! I don't give a flying
shit what you people are selling! You've people
have been <u>harassing</u> me for the past month and a
half!

As the snake slithers up Anne's leg, beads of sweat form over Anne's face. She
fidgets in her chair, then clears her throat, carefully swallowing the dry lump.

ANNE
Well...I...I truly apologize for the inconvenience,
Ms. Corset.

The snake makes its way toward Anne's groin.

MS. CORSET (V.O.)
Get a fucking life!

The sharp CLICK forces Anne to remove her headset...

Anne stands from the chair. The snake is gone.

Or, was it even there to begin with?

With a slackened expression on her face, she frantically surveys the busy office. Then, she reaches for a photo in the top desk drawer. Stares at it.

The photo is of Anne at graduation; however, she is much heavier (at least a hundred pounds heavier). Her foster parents, HAROLD and MOLLY, both Jewish, proudly stand next to Anne, who is dressed in a red cap and gown, and smiling too.

Anne wipes the tears from her eyes, grabs her purse, and exits the cubicle.

INT. OFFICE, USR - CONTINUOUS

Anne hurries to the LADIES RESTROOM, passing Jamie who is flirting with TOM, the office stud, next to the vending machine. Tries to open the door, but the door is locked. She turns toward the MENS sign.

INT. MEN'S RESTROOM, USR - CONTINUOUS

The restroom is empty; however, Anne doesn't care anyway as she hurries to the first sink and splashes her face with cold water; and while doing so, one of her contacts springs out.

Anne shuts off the water and plugs the sink before the contact falls into the drain. She runs her finger across the sink until she comes across a round object, the contact!

As she picks up the contact and holds it close to her good eye, she squints her left eye and focuses with the right.

The contact isn't flimsy as before; instead, it's hard like glass.

Anne places the contact between her fingers, index and thumb, which causes the contact to suddenly break in half!

The sudden break pricks her thumb, drawing a drop of blood.

Anne walks to the stall. Grabs a square of toilet paper.

With one eye closed, Anne wraps her finger in the toilet paper and leaves the stall.

As she makes her way to the sink, she hears flesh smacking against flesh. The sound, Anne pinpoints, coming from the last stall.

She directs her eyes to the reflection in the reflection, the man's two legs spread open underneath the stall's door, pants pulled down to his ankles; and the man's panting too, like a dog.

EXT. CORPORATE BUILDING - DAY

Anne, now wearing black rimmed glasses, not contacts, and still pale and weak from the previous panic attack, exits through the revolving door.

EXT. PARKING LOT - CONTINUOUS

As Anne inserts the car key into the lock, her eyes come across a golf ball size dent with a sliver of red paint on the door.

Anne looks to the car next to hers: a red smartcar. Shakes her head in disgust.

As Anne opens the car door, her eyes cross another car -- the same black Lincoln from earlier parked at the other end of the parking lot.

INT. FITNESS CITY - DAY

The gym is fairly quiet, only a couple of businessmen squeezing in a quick workout after work.

Dressed in her daily workout getup, purple tanktop, black spandex pants, hair held in a ponytail by a black barrette, Anne steps off the ELLIPTICAL, then catches her breath, then wipes down the machine with a clean towel.

A YOUNG MAN, a few years younger than Anne, white, ripped, follows suit and wipes down the machine next to hers.

As Anne turns around to grab her water bottle from the holster, she turns back around toward the young man, only to find his wandering eyes settled on the tattoo of a BLACK CONSTRICTOR stretching down her back right shoulder.

Blushing a little, Anne makes eye contact with the young man. The half side of Anne's face lifts with a smile, small and subtle and yet distinguishable -- both eyes glistening faintly.

>   ANNE
>   Hi.

>   YOUNG MAN
>   Nice tattoo.

>   ANNE
>   Oh! Thanks.

The silence builds, now awkward. The smile dissolves from Anne's face, as the young man walks away.

Embarrassed, Anne grabs her things and walks to the TREADMILL stationed across the room, turning her shoulder once during the walk, only to find the young man nowhere around.

As she steps onto the treadmill, her attention is drawn to the two men laughing in front of the dumbbells. One of them is the same young man from before. The other, a BLACK MAN dressed in spandex, older and ripped as well.

The black man is touching Jason's bicep, then Jason smiles, eyes glistening.

Anne scowls and increases the speed on the treadmill.

INT. HALLWAY, FITNESS CITY - NIGHT

Exhausted from the intense workout, Anne sits with her back against the wall and googles the words, "TATTOO REMOVAL" on her smartphone.

163

The door to the WOMEN'S LOCKER ROOM opens with a loud SQUEAK!

Anne removes her eyes from the smartphone, grabs her things, and stands up. An uppity WOMAN exits.

> WOMAN
> She's all yours, Anne.

> ANNE
> Thanks.

INT. LOCKER ROOM, FITNESS CITY - NIGHT

All of the SHOWERS are empty, except for one.

In the middle of a cloud of steam stands Anne underneath the running shower faucet tucked away in the far corner.

Quickly and yet precisely, Anne washes the shampoo from her hair.

As the hot water runs over Anne's face, a sudden SQUEAK cuts through the locker room!

Anne opens her eyes, shoots her attention toward the lockers across the room.

Carefully, Anne turns off the water. Another SQUEAK, sharper now like two hinges grating against one another.

Anne shields one hand over her groin while she grabs the towel from the hanger with the other hand, and then wraps it around her torso.

With her body now covered, Anne grabs her glasses from the soap holder and steps from the shower.

Anne sees two shadows slinking across the wall behind the lockers. Both eyes, honing...

A single DROP of water cast from a faucet pulls her narrow eyes toward the set of mirrors across the locker room.

Anne catches her reflection; however, the image of her is distorted. The steam from the showers has fogged up all mirrors, expect for one. Her body, much thinner too, ghastly, the skin scaly.

As Anne puts on her glasses, a stabbing pain runs through her eyes, causing her to cringe in agony.

The mirror suddenly cracks, then the right side of the frame cracks, causing Anne to slip over the wet tile.

During the fall, Anne's left wrist catches most of the fall.

INT. TRAINER'S OFFICE - NIGHT

Dressed in her work clothes, her hair still damp from the previous shower, Anne sits with her left arm draped over a man's legs, which are the size of tree trunks.

The legs belong to the gym's primary trainer, RICK, 40's, heavily tanned, and, of course, ripped.

> RICK
> Happens to the best of us, Anne.

As Rick finishes the final touches on Anne's wrist, he looks down at the broken glasses in Anne's hand.

> RICK (CONT'D)
> Every once in a while, we get a flat tire...
> (shrugging)
> ...The solution is an easy one: we fix it.

> ANNE
> (depressingly)
> I wish it was that simple...

Rick lowers his head into Anne's range of vision.

> RICK
> Well, sometimes, the most complicated things
> turn out to be the most simple.

INT. ANNE'S HONDA CIVIC - NIGHT

Anne's eyes turn toward the two headlights in the rear view mirror.

The car is too dark to make out from the darkness of night and the lack of streetlights; nonetheless, the suspicious car keeps its distance.

INT. ANNE'S KITCHEN - NIGHT

Anne places a TV dinner into the microwave -- one of those low fat cordon bleus with a side of green beans -- and sets the timer to three minutes.

INT. ANNE'S BEDROOM - CONTINUOUS

While the dinner cooks, Anne dresses in more appropriate attire: a long white tee that stretches halfway down her thighs.

Anne fishes out an old pair of reading glasses from the nightstand. They're ugly things, very how-would-she-say, "old fashioned," but they do the trick.

INT. ANNE'S KITCHEN - CONTINUOUS

Anne vacantly stares at the timer on the microwave as it counts down to zero.

INT. ANNE'S BEDROOM - NIGHT

Anne stands in front of a mirror and stares at the old scars on her body, a long pink jagged one that stretched all the way up the right side of her ribcage, and then a vertical scar, as narrow as a blade, along her upper abdomen.

INT. ANNE'S BATHROOM - NIGHT

Anne places a glass of red wine on the floor and eases herself into the warm bubbly water in the bathtub covered in scented candles and other fragrances, mostly eucalyptus.

As Anne oozes farther down into the tub, she raises her leg and applies shaving cream, starting from her ankle to her thigh. She grabs a razor. Slides the blade along her leg the same way she applied cream: from her ankle to her thigh.

A sudden tug of the blade over her skin!

                    ANNE
        Ouch!

The blade pops from the mount and falls into the water.

Anne sits upright. Caresses the sore spot on her leg. Pulls her hand away, then a
sliver of skin. Looks closely at the piece of skin between her fingertips. It's hard
and round, similar to the scale of a snake...

Anne lifts her leg from the water and checks her skin. There's no bruise, no cut,
no blood, no mark on her body.

With confusion, she searches for the blade at the bottom of the tub. Finds it.
Pulls it close. Stares. Gently presses the blade against her pale wrist...

                    ANNE (V.O.) (CONT'D)
            I always wondered why I was drawn to certain
            things...

INT. DISCOVERY ZONE - DAY - FLASHBACK SEQUENCE

Anne stands in front of the aquarium and watches the jellyfish swimming before
her eyes. She looks down at the newspaper in her hands. Stares at Steven Price's
face in the OBITUARY section.

INT. OFFICE, USR - DAY - FLASHBACK SEQUENCE

As Anne stands outside Jamie's cubicle, she turns her shoulder and witnesses Dave
stalking closer. A grin on his face.

                    ANNE (V.O.)
            ...why certain gestures stayed with me the most...

INT. ANNE'S CUBICLE - DAY - FLASHBACK SEQUENCE

A snake slithers up Anne's leg.

                    ANNE (V.O.)
        ...feelings.

INT. PARKING LOT - DAY - FLASHBACK SEQUENCE

Anne opens the car door. Her eyes keenly drawn to the mysterious black Lincoln parked across the parking lot.

> ANNE (V.O.)
> Were these everyday occurrences trying to tell me something?

INT. ANNE'S BEDROOM - NIGHT - FLASHBACK SEQUENCE

Anne stands in front of the mirror. Naked. Carefully, she stares at the scar on the side of her body.

> ANNE (V.O.)
> Were they helping me remember?

EXT. ANNE'S HOUSE - NIGHT - PRESENT DAY

We see two strange men exiting the same black Lincoln. We don't see their faces; however, we see the guns held down by their waist side.

> ANNE (V.O.)
> I don't know what it was I was trying to remember.

In SLOW MOTION, we see the two men approaching Anne's house.

INT. ANNE'S BATHROOM - NIGHT

Anne stares at the razor pressed against her wrist.

> ANNE (V.O.)
> I had to remember.

Slowly, Anne draws her eyes upward to us; and that is when we see her eyes sharpen like blades.

FADE TO BLACK.

AND NOW A SNEAK PEEK
FROM THE FINAL CHAPTER
OF THE *HARD SERIES*...

FADE IN:

EXT. ATLANTIC OCEAN - NIGHT

The body of a young GIRL, around nine years old, suddenly CRASHES into the ocean water. Her lifeless body sinks farther and farther into a dark abyss.

As she sinks toward the bottom of the ocean, we see her eyes gradually open, revealing her all white eyes -- ANNE'S eyes! Then a strange pink light shines on Anne's face.

> MERROTTI (V.O.)
> The only way to destroy a monster, Chloe, is to become one.

We hear the slide-action of an automatic handgun swiftly cocking over the blackness.

INT. LIVING ROOM, MERROTTI'S HOUSE - NIGHT

The rogue detective, DEVON MERROTTI, 50's, holds the handgun in front of CHLOE, now 26 years old, formerly known as the troubled foster child, Anne Roth.

> MERROTTI
> (to Chloe)
> Are you ready?

                                                            JUMP CUT TO:

EXT. DOWNTOWN JACKSON, MISSISSIPPI - NIGHT

We see an overhead view of Jackson, each building lit up in the night darkness. The streets, empty.

INT. MERROTTI'S CAR - DAY

Chloe, same age, sits in the passenger seat. Her sharp eyes focused on the house across the street. Poised. Next to her sits Merrotti, poised as well.

> MALE'S VOICE (V.O.)
> Our history is tragic...

INT. MARCUS'S CAR - DAY

Seated by the steering wheel is MARCUS HOPKINS, now in his 60's, has a scar on the side of his face. His eyes focused on Anne's foster parent's house.

EXT. JUNGLE, COLUMBIA - DAY

Leon's former butler, DIEGO, fifteen years old, known as the "Jungle Spider," face and hands covered in blood, dashes around the trees. Behind him, a cartel armed to the teeth chases him. Rifles drawn on him. Diego, ducking and dodging each bullet.

> MALE'S VOICE (V.O.)
> ...Violent...

EXT. STREET, SUBURBS - NIGHT

The controversial journalist, RENNY JACOBSON, ten years old, face covered in black soot, breathing heavily, stands in front of a flaming house. Tiny flames growing in his eyes.

> MALE'S VOICE (V.O.)
> ...Sad...

INT. TRAINING ROOM, AERODYNE - DAY

A young Indian doctor, DHAWAN, holds hands with young Chloe, six years old, a couple of years before adoption. Both of them running from a team of armed GUARDS.

> MALE'S VOICE (V.O.)
> ...optimistic.

INT. CHLOE'S BEDROOM - NIGHT

A lanky man, LOUIS BRINGER, belt in hand, walks into the bedroom where Chloe, now eleven years old, scurries to the corner. Shields her body.

> MALE'S VOICE (V.O.)
> After everything he had put you through...

INT. LIVING ROOM, BRINGER'S HOUSE - DAY

Merrotti kicks open a basement door, handgun gripped tightly in hand.

INT. BASEMENT, BRINGER'S HOUSE - DAY

Chloe prowls down a dark hallway.

> MALE'S VOICE (V.O.)
> ...you had a chance to redirect the course of
> history.

INT. BUNGALOW, MORACCO - DAY

On the porch, Merrotti and Chloe (both a couple of years older) watch the sun rise over the breathtaking view of mountains. Merrotti places his hand over Chloe's hand.

INT. THE DUNGEON, BRINGER'S HOUSE - DAY

With the handgun kept close to his body, Merrotti creeps around a corner; and there, in the dungeon filled with sexual toys, we see over a dozen malnourished GIRLS, ranging from ten to twelve years old, huddled in the corner of the room like a colony.

INT. CAMP DELTA - NIGHT

Chloe, drenching wet, waits in the bushes. Her breath, extremely heavy.

> MALE'S VOICE (V.O.)
> Yet, you failed to see the devil on your shoulder.

EXT. COW PASTURE - DAY

A frightened man, LOUIS BRINGER, scrambles through the field, turning his shoulder toward Merrotti and Chloe, both casually stalking him.

> MALE'S VOICE (V.O.)
> Tell me, Chloe. Why didn't you kill him?

EXT. GROVE - DAY

Louis Bringer crawls away from Merrotti and Chloe. We CLOSE IN on Chloe, who looms over Bringer's weak body.

> CHLOE (V.O.)
> Killing him would be...

INT. INTERROGATION ROOM, JENECORP - DAY

In a stale white room sits Chloe. She's much older, now well into her 60's. She has two scars in the shape of tiny dots underneath both of her eyes. Her hair, all white. Eyebrows as well, white.

In front of her patiently sits the man behind the voice, MARK, an android, dressed in a fancy white suit.

Chloe moves her head upward, her eyes piercing.

> CHLOE
> (to Mark)
> ...Too easy.

INT. CORRIDOR, JENECORP - DAY

A team of armed AGENTS -- dressed in white gear, white guns as well -- walk Chloe to her cell. Both of her hands bound by shackles. A black bag worn over her head.

INT. HALLWAY, JENECORP - DAY

Two men, one head scientist, PARK, and the other, Agent NOBLE, stroll toward a room surrounded by glass.

                              PARK (V.O.)
            With our new operating system, we will be able
            to control the entire world...

INT. OVAL OFFICE - DAY

The President, BILL LOCKHART (Junior) stands behind the window
overlooking the front lawn of the White House. His CHAUFFEUR sits on the
couch behind him -- the right side of its artificial face automatically closes over its
robotic face.

INT. SERVER ROOM, JENECORP - DAY

Both Park and Noble stand in front of a glass box connected to a conveyer belt,
which is connected to two massive servers.

                                PARK
                             (to Noble)
                   ...with one click of a button.

INT. HALLWAY, JENECORP - DAY

Park and Noble face each other.

                               NOBLE
                  What about the rest of her body?

                                PARK
                  It's simple. All we need is her head...

INT. OBSERVATIONAL ROOM, JENECORP - DAY

The ENGINEER pushes the ENTER key on the keyboard.

                            ENGINEER (V.O.)
                         Let the show begin...

INT. CHLOE'S CELL, JENECORP - DAY

Chloe sits on the edge of her bed, head hanging toward the floor.

EXT. LAKE ATITLÁN - DAY

With her back facing us, Chloe, late 20's, walks to the edge of the bluff overlooking the lake.

BLACK SCREEN

SUPER: "A Woman Bound By Misery."

EXT. PIRATE'S COVE - DAY

As the sun sets over the ocean, Chloe, 24, drops to her knees as she cradles her dead father, LEON, in her arms.

EXT. SCRAPYARD - NIGHT

Chloe, late 20's, rushes down a steep hill and discovers her stepsister, SALLY, five years old, lying dead in the garbage. Cradles her body. Crying.

EXT. CAMP DELTA - NIGHT

In the pouring rain, Merrotti sits on his knees, black bag worn over his head, hands tied behind his back. A team of AGENTS surround the detective.

Agent BALSTAR stands behind Merrotti with a pistol pressed against his head.

EXT. WOODS, LEATHERBY MANOR - DAY

Kneeled on the ground, Chloe pulls out a pair of dove figurines from the small chest buried in the soil.

BLACK SCREEN

SUPER: "Bound By Rage."

EXT. FOOD MARKETS, HONG KONG - NIGHT

Chloe prowls through the crowded markets, stalking two AGENTS sent by JeneCorp (The Company).

INT. HALLWAY, APARTMENT - DAY

Chloe, 26, dressed in only her underwear, twirls around Agent KARP, then smashes his face into the wall. Gazes the next AGENT. Eyes white. Mouth gaping.

INT. CONTROL ROOM, AERODYNE - NIGHT

With a shotgun in hand, a GUARD fires off one shot after another while backpedaling into a dark corner. Behind him, a pair of white eyes -- Chloe's eyes -- light up in the shadows.

BLACK SCREEN

SUPER: "Bound By Betrayal."

EXT. LEATHERBY MANOR - NIGHT

Diego, 70's, militarized, strolls from the flaming mansion to the idle helicopter -- a bag carrying Medusa's head in one gloved hand, a gun in the other.

INT. HIDEOUT, VENEZUELA - NIGHT

A team of AGENTS led by Agent Noble storm through the dark hallways.

INT. INTERROGATION ROOM, JENECORP - DAY

Agent Noble stands over Chloe's weak body, revealing his augmented arm: his metal fingers curling into a fist.

INT. BEDROOM, HIDEOUT - NIGHT

As Diego, now bald, still in his 70's, stands in front of the window, he places the Medusa scale on the tip of his tongue.

BLACK SCREEN

SUPER: "Bound By Science."

EXT. STREETS, HONG KONG - NIGHT

Chloe stands at the edge of the sidewalk outside a busy intersection and gazes the streetlight -- her eyes rapidly flickering over white.

EXT. DIRT ROAD, EL SALVADOR - DAY

As Chloe swerves the motorcycle away from the SUV, she directs her deadly gaze toward the GPS device on the SUV's dashboard, the electronics of the SUV causing the vehicle to suddenly flip in the air!

INT. INTERROGATION ROOM, JENECORP - DAY

Agent Noble pulls Chloe closer and grabs her by the throat with his good hand. Squeezes tighter.

Chloe scowls, teeth clenched.

                    CHLOE
          No matter what happens to me, I will destroy
          you.

SERIES OF SHOTS - THE AFTERMATH

-- The skyline of Jackson is filled with rising flames.

-- Large cities from New York to Los Angeles remain covered in a blanket of ash.

-- We see a pedestrian on the sidewalk, covered in stone, standing like a statue, smartphone in hand...

EXT. RUINS - DAY

Cloaked in rags of clothing, as well as a long spear gripped in his holey gloved hand, A YOUNG MAN steps onto a sturdy chunk of rumble left behind from a demolished building.

                    MARK (V.O.)
          History has a funny way of repeating itself.

We see the back of the young man, Chloe's son, AARON, early 40's, looking out into a gray horizon plagued with destruction.

CHLOE (V.O.)
I thought your kind didn't have a sense of humor.

INT. INTERROGATION ROOM, JENECORP - DAY

Mark cracks a smile on his hollow face. Then, in a SERIES OF QUICK
SHOTS, we see Chloe ripping off Marks's head and then throwing its head
through the mirror, shattering the glass to pieces...

HARD

JUSTICE

STARRING STEPHANIE GRAFT AS "CHLOE" AND HUGO RAMIREZ AS "DIEGO" IN HARD JUSTICE

DIRECTED BY MEMPHIS BLACK   PRODUCED BY DON GREENE   CO PRODUCED BY THOMAS LEVINE   EXECUTIVE PRODUCER HAILEY SCHUBERT

SCREENPLAY BY WILLIAM S. MITCHAM   BASED ON THE NOVEL BY ELLIS KROSS   A RED CLAW PRODUCTION

www.ingramcontent.com/pod-product-compliance
Lightning Source LLC
Chambersburg PA
CBHW050936120626
46552CB00001B/230